THE ECHO OF SILENCE

THE ECHO OF SILENCE

Some secrets never stay buried

Geoffrey Kneller

Copyright © 2025 by Geoffrey Kneller

All rights reserved. No part of this publication may be reproduced, distributed, or transmitted in any form or by any means, including photocopying, recording, or other electronic or mechanical methods, without the prior written permission of the publisher, except in the case of brief quotations embodied in critical reviews and certain other noncommercial uses permitted by copyright law.

This is a work of fiction. Names, characters, places, and incidents either are the products of the author's imagination or are used fictitiously. Any resemblance to actual persons, living or dead, businesses, companies, events, or locales is entirely coincidental.

First Edition: May 2025

Praise for Geoffrey Kneller

"One of the most compelling voices in contemporary mystery fiction." — The Boston Literary Review

"Kneller's atmospheric prose and intricate plotting set a new standard for psychological thrillers." — Mystery Writers Guild

"Few authors capture the essence of small-town secrets like Geoffrey Kneller." — Suspense Magazine

"A master of psychological tension and environmental themes." — The New England Book Critic

"Kneller weaves complex mysteries that linger in the mind long after the final page." — Thriller Authors Association

For those who seek truth in the silence.

Acknowledgments

To the readers who have walked with me through the shadows of countless mysteries, your unwavering support has been my guiding light in the darkest of narratives. My profound gratitude to the editorial team whose relentless pursuit of perfection has shaped this story into something far greater than I could have imagined alone. Your insights cut through the fog of creation like a lighthouse beam. To the brave souls of coastal communities who shared their stories of environmental devastation with unflinching honesty—your resilience in the face of corporate indifference has forever altered my understanding of justice. And to those who have stood beside me through the tempests of creation and the calm waters of completion—you know who you are, and so does my heart.

Table of Contents

Chapter 1: The Archives

Chapter 2: The Pattern

Chapter 3: The Victims

Chapter 4: The Warning

Chapter 5: The Doubt

Chapter 6: The Connection

Chapter 7: The Storm

Chapter 8: The Truth

Chapter 9: The Reckoning

Chapter 10: The Aftermath

Chapter 1: The Archives

The basement of the Maplewood Bay Police Department smelled of mildew and forgotten promises. Detective Eliza Morgan sneezed as another plume of dust rose from the cardboard box she'd just pulled from the metal shelving unit. The harsh fluorescent lighting cast everything in a sickly pallor, including her own hands, pale from too many hours indoors during what should have been summer's final hurrah.

"Bless you!" called a voice from somewhere beyond the maze of shelves. "That's seventeen today. I'm keeping count."

Eliza smiled despite her frustration. "Thanks for the statistics, Davis," she called back to the department's records clerk. "Maybe instead of counting my sneezes, you could help me with these boxes?"

"No can do, Detective. Chief's orders—you're the only one authorized to handle the cold cases. Something about your 'special brain.'"

Eliza sighed. Her "special brain"—her photographic memory—was both blessing and curse. It had earned her the fastest detective promotion in department history, but it also meant she got stuck with jobs like this: digitizing thirty years of cold case files before the department relocated to their new, smaller building next month.

She placed the dusty box on a metal table and opened it carefully. Inside were the forgotten remnants of someone's tragedy: Case #87-114, missing person, presumed dead. Melissa Canning, age 26, disappeared October 1987. Eliza didn't need to read the file to remember the details—she'd reviewed it briefly last week. Nursing student, vanished after a night shift, car found at the scenic overlook above the bay, no signs of struggle, no body ever recovered.

The official theory: suicide by drowning. The evidence: a history of depression, a recent breakup, and a prescription for antidepressants found in her apartment. Case effectively closed without being solved.

Eliza began methodically photographing each document with the department's digital scanner. The process was mind-numbing, but necessary. Budget cuts meant downsizing, and the new building had no space for the physical archives. Everything had to be digitized or placed in deep storage at the county facility.

"Hey, Morgan." Detective James Harlow appeared at the end of the row, his broad shoulders nearly touching both shelves. At fifty-three, he was the department veteran, her mentor, and the only one who never seemed impressed or intimidated by her memory. "Still buried in the land of the forgotten?"

"Quite literally." She held up a dust-covered evidence bag containing a woman's scarf. "This hasn't seen daylight since the first Bush administration."

James leaned against the shelf. "Chief Wallace is asking about your progress. The moving company needs a timeline."

"Tell him I'm on box forty-seven of approximately three hundred." She gestured to the seemingly endless rows of shelving. "At current pace, I should be done by retirement age."

"That good, huh?" James chuckled. "Need any help? I could spare an hour before my shift ends."

"Thanks, but apparently my 'special brain' is required." She tapped her temple. "Besides, you'd just slow me down with all your questions. I've already memorized most of these files."

"Show-off." His tone was affectionate. James was one of the few who treated her memory as simply another tool, not a parlor trick or an alienating oddity.

"It's not showing off if it's useful." Eliza turned back to her scanning. "Did you need something specific, or just checking that I haven't suffocated under an avalanche of cold cases?"

"Bit of both. Also, thought you might want to know we got a hit on the Parkman burglaries. Fingerprint match came back on those jewelry store break-ins."

"Let me guess—Ronnie Decker?"

James raised an eyebrow. "How'd you know?"

"The tool marks on the security gate matched the ones from the Marina break-in three years ago. Ronnie did eighteen months for that one, got out in April. Plus, he always hits jewelry stores on the first Tuesday of the month—something about delivery schedules."

James shook his head. "Sometimes it's downright spooky working with you."

"Not spooky. Just observant." Eliza turned back to her scanning. "Go arrest Ronnie. I'll be here, communing with the ghosts."

After James left, Eliza fell into a rhythm. Scan, save, next page. The monotony allowed her mind to wander through the details of each case, connecting fragments that no one had bothered to connect before. Most were straightforward—domestic disputes turned deadly, robberies gone wrong, drug deals with predictably tragic endings.

But some—like Melissa Canning's—left questions that nagged at her. The suicide theory had always seemed too convenient. According to the file, Melissa had just been accepted to an advanced nursing program and had made plans to visit her sister the following weekend. Not typical behavior for someone planning to end their life.

Eliza finished with Melissa's box and reached for the next one. Case #92-073. Another missing person: Thomas Reeves, 34, high school history teacher, disappeared May 1992. His car found abandoned at Maplewood State Park, hiking trail entrance. No signs of struggle. Never found.

As she scanned his file, something caught her eye—a photograph of personal effects found in his car. Keys, wallet, hiking boots... and a small carved wooden bird, positioned on the passenger seat.

Something about that bird triggered a connection in Eliza's memory. She paused, letting her mind retrieve the image that was bothering her. Then it clicked—Melissa Canning's file had mentioned a small personal item left behind too. A silver charm bracelet with only one charm—a tiny bird—found on the guardrail at the overlook.

Coincidence, probably. But Eliza's instincts hummed. She pulled Melissa's file back out and confirmed—yes, a bird charm. Different material but similar positioning—left in a visible place, as if deliberately placed rather than accidentally dropped.

"Huh," she murmured to herself.

She continued working, but now with heightened attention. Three boxes later, she found another one: Case #97-221. Katherine Winters, 41, real estate agent, disappeared September 1997. Car found at the marina, boat missing, presumed boating accident. Personal effects included a small ceramic bird figurine on the dock beside her slip.

Eliza's pulse quickened. Three cases, spanning a decade, with the same unusual detail—a bird-shaped object left behind. And something else—she checked the dates again. 1987, 1992, 1997. Five years between each disappearance.

She quickly moved through more boxes, scanning for similar cases. Within an hour, she'd found two more:

Case #02-156: Daniel Foster, 38, accountant, disappeared November 2002. Car found at trailhead of coastal hiking path. Small metal bird paperweight on dashboard.

Case #07-089: Sarah Lindstrom, 29, librarian, disappeared August 2007. Car found in grocery store parking lot after closing. Small glass bird figurine on ground beside driver's door.

Five cases. Five disappearances. Five bird tokens. Each five years apart.

Eliza sat back, her mind racing. This couldn't be coincidence. She checked the case assignments—different detectives had handled each investigation, none making the connection to the others. Each case had been treated as isolated, with various theories: suicide, accident, possible voluntary disappearance.

But Eliza saw the pattern now. And if the pattern held...the next disappearance would have been in 2012, and another would be due this year—2017.

She quickly searched for a 2012 case, finding it after twenty minutes of digging:

Case #12-204: Michael Reynolds, 45, journalist, disappeared October 2012. Car found at beach parking lot. Small wooden bird carving on sea wall nearby.

Six cases. Thirty years. No bodies ever found.

Eliza gathered the files and spread them across the table. She began creating a timeline, noting similarities beyond the bird tokens. All disappearances occurred during rainy weather. All vehicles were found with no signs of struggle. All victims were well-regarded in the community with no obvious enemies.

And something else—she flipped through the interview transcripts. Three of the victims had recently mentioned to friends or family that they were "looking into something important." Two had scheduled appointments with the same psychologist—Dr. Nathan Wells.

Eliza froze. Dr. Wells. Her mother's fiancé. The man who had been like a father to her since her own father's death fifteen years ago.

"No," she whispered. "That's not possible."

But her perfect memory wouldn't let her dismiss the connection. Dr. Wells had been practicing in Maplewood Bay for over thirty years. He was the town's most respected psychologist, treating everyone from troubled teens to the mayor himself. He was a pillar of the community, a man above suspicion.

And he was about to become her stepfather.

Eliza's phone buzzed with a text message. She glanced down to see Nathan's name on the screen: "Your mother and I are making lasagna tonight. Coming for dinner? 7pm."

As she stared at the message, a chill ran through her that had nothing to do with the basement's perpetual dampness. She looked back at the files spread before her—at thirty years of unsolved disappearances connected by tiny bird tokens and five-year intervals.

If the pattern held, someone would disappear this year. Soon.

Her phone buzzed again: "Eliza? Dinner tonight?"

She texted back: "Yes. See you at 7."

Then she carefully gathered the files and began making copies. Whatever was happening in Maplewood Bay had gone unnoticed for three decades. But not anymore. Not now that she had seen the pattern.

Not now that she had heard the echo of silence left by six missing people—and the soft, ominous ticking of a five-year clock about to chime again.

Chapter 2: The Pattern

Eliza Morgan's mother had always said that lasagna could solve most of life's problems. As steam rose from the ceramic dish at the center of the dining table, Eliza wished that were true. The rich aroma of tomato sauce, herbs, and melted cheese filled the cozy dining room of her mother's Victorian home, but even comfort food couldn't quiet the questions swirling in her mind.

"You've barely touched your food," said Patricia Morgan, reaching across to touch her daughter's hand. At sixty-two, Patricia still possessed the warm beauty that had made her the town's most beloved elementary school teacher for three decades. "Are you feeling alright?"

"Just tired," Eliza replied, forcing a smile. "I've been stuck in the basement archives all week."

"Ah, the famous cold case digitization project," said Dr. Nathan Wells from across the table. He cut his lasagna into precise squares, methodical as always. "Finding anything interesting down there in the department's graveyard?"

Eliza studied him carefully. At sixty-five, Nathan was distinguished rather than handsome—silver hair always perfectly combed, wire-rimmed glasses perched on an aquiline nose, posture military-straight even at the dinner table. He'd been her mother's fiancé for two years, and had known their family for much longer—since before her father's death.

"Mostly routine cases," she said, watching his reaction. "Though I did notice some patterns no one had connected before."

"Patterns are your specialty, aren't they?" Nathan smiled, his eyes crinkling at the corners. "That remarkable memory of yours—seeing connections others miss."

Was there something in his tone? A slight tension? Or was she projecting her own sudden suspicions?

"It's just data," Eliza said, deliberately casual. "Anyone could see it if they looked at all the cases together."

"But no one ever does," Nathan replied. "That's the beauty of your work, Eliza. You see the whole picture where others only see fragments."

Patricia beamed. "Nathan's always been your biggest fan, honey. He was just telling Mayor Whitaker at the charity gala last week how the department doesn't appreciate your full potential."

"The mayor," Eliza said, filing away this connection. "You two are close?"

"We serve on several community boards together," Nathan said. "Richard's been instrumental in the waterfront redevelopment project."

The same waterfront where Katherine Winters had disappeared in 1997, Eliza thought.

"How's the wedding planning coming along?" she asked, deliberately changing the subject.

Patricia brightened. "We've finally settled on October 15th. The foliage should be perfect, and we've booked the Bayview Hotel for the reception."

October. When Michael Reynolds had disappeared in 2012. When Melissa Canning had vanished in 1987.

"That's... during storm season," Eliza said carefully.

"We're hoping for one of those perfect autumn days," Nathan said. "But the hotel has a lovely indoor option if the weather turns."

Rain. All six disappearances had occurred during rainy weather.

"Speaking of weather," Nathan continued, "I heard there's a major system coming through next weekend. Might be the first big storm of the season."

Eliza's fork froze halfway to her mouth. Next weekend would mark exactly five years since Michael Reynolds' disappearance.

"Eliza?" Her mother was looking at her with concern. "You went pale. Are you sure you're feeling well?"

"Fine," she managed. "Just remembered I left some files unsecured at the station."

Nathan studied her with professional interest. "You seem tense tonight. Is something bothering you? Work stress, perhaps?"

The psychologist's gaze was penetrating, and Eliza felt suddenly exposed, as if he could read her thoughts. Had he always watched her this closely, or was she now hyper-aware of his attention?

"Nothing specific," she lied. "The department move has everyone on edge."

"Change is always stressful," he nodded sagely. "Even positive change."

After dinner, as Patricia cleared the plates, Nathan followed Eliza onto the back porch. The night air was cool, carrying the salt scent of the bay. In the distance, the lighthouse beam swept across the water in rhythmic pulses.

"I've been meaning to ask you something," Nathan said, leaning against the porch railing beside her.

Eliza's muscles tensed. "Oh?"

"Your mother is worried about you. Says you've been distant lately. Working too much."

"The job demands it."

"Of course." He nodded. "But I wonder if there's something else. You have that look you used to get as a teenager when something was troubling you."

"What look is that?"

"Like you're solving a puzzle no one else can see." He smiled. "Your father had the same expression when he was working on a difficult case."

The mention of her father sent a pang through her chest. Thomas Morgan had been the department's most respected detective before his fatal car accident fifteen years ago—an accident that had occurred on the same coastal road where Thomas Reeves' car had been found in 1992.

"I didn't realize you knew my father that well," she said carefully.

"We weren't close friends, but in a town this size, our paths crossed often. Professional courtesy between a detective and a psychologist." Nathan's expression softened. "He was very proud of you, you know. Said you'd be a better detective than he ever was."

Eliza swallowed hard. "I should get going. Early shift tomorrow."

"Of course." Nathan straightened. "Oh, before you go—I've been meaning to return something to you."

He reached into his pocket and withdrew a small object, holding it out in his palm. A small silver bird charm.

Eliza's blood turned to ice.

"Found this in the guest room after you stayed over last month," Nathan explained. "Thought it might be yours."

With a trembling hand, Eliza took the charm. It was similar to the one described in Melissa Canning's file, but not identical. This one was a sparrow, not the robin described in the evidence log.

"Thanks," she managed. "It's... from an old bracelet."

Nathan nodded, seemingly satisfied. "Drive safely. The fog's rolling in."

Back in her car, Eliza sat gripping the steering wheel, the bird charm clutched in her palm so tightly it left an impression. Coincidence? A deliberate message? Or was she seeing connections that weren't there?

She started the engine and pulled away from her mother's house, watching Nathan's silhouette in the rearview mirror as he stood on the porch, watching her leave.

The next morning, Eliza arrived at the station before dawn. The building was nearly empty—just the night shift dispatcher and a couple of patrol officers finishing their reports. Perfect.

She made her way to the basement, unlocking the storage room she'd claimed as her workspace. Inside, she'd created a timeline on a forgotten corkboard, connecting the six disappearances with red string. Photos of the victims formed a row across the top, while beneath them she'd pinned weather reports, interview transcripts, and evidence logs.

Now she added new elements: Nathan's connections to the victims she knew about, the mayor's name, the waterfront development project, and notes about her father's accident. The pattern was expanding, becoming more complex.

She stepped back, studying the board. If she was right—if these disappearances were connected, if they were not accidents or suicides but something more sinister—then someone had been operating undetected in Maplewood Bay for thirty years. Someone with the influence to make investigations go away. Someone trusted by the community.

Someone like Nathan?

The thought made her stomach clench. Nathan, who had counseled her through her grief after her father's death. Nathan, who made her mother happier than she'd been in years. Nathan, who had just handed her a bird charm with a casual explanation.

"What are you doing here so early?"

Eliza jumped, spinning around to find James Harlow in the doorway, holding two coffee cups.

"Jesus, James! You scared me."

"Sorry." He handed her one of the coffees. "Saw your car outside. Figured you could use this." His eyes moved past her to the corkboard. "What's all this?"

Eliza hesitated. James had been her mentor since she joined the force, the one person who had always believed in her. But this was different. This was accusing a respected community member—her future stepfather—of potentially being involved in multiple disappearances.

"I found something in the cold cases," she said finally. "A pattern no one noticed before."

James stepped closer to the board, coffee forgotten. His eyes narrowed as he took in the connections she'd mapped.

"Six disappearances, five years apart," he read aloud. "Bird tokens at each scene." He turned to her. "And you think they're connected?"

"The statistical probability of six unrelated cases sharing these specific characteristics is virtually zero."

"Okay, but what's this?" He pointed to Nathan's name, which she'd written with a question mark.

Eliza took a deep breath. "Three of the victims had appointments with Dr. Wells shortly before they disappeared. And he knew my father, who died on the same road where one victim's car was found."

James's expression darkened. "Eliza, that's a serious implication. Dr. Wells has been in this town forever. He's treated half the population at some point."

"I know how it sounds."

"Do you? Because it sounds like you're suggesting your mother's fiancé might be involved in multiple disappearances."

"I'm not suggesting anything yet. I'm just... mapping connections."

James ran a hand through his graying hair. "Look, I trust your instincts. You see things others miss. But this is thin, even for a preliminary theory."

"That's why I need your help," Eliza said. "I need to dig deeper, but I can't do it officially. Not without more evidence."

"And not when it involves your future stepfather," James added.

"Exactly."

James studied the board again, his detective's mind clearly processing the information. "What about Chief Wallace? He was around for some of these cases."

"Wallace was the responding officer on the Melissa Canning case in '87," Eliza confirmed. "He ruled it a probable suicide within forty-eight hours."

"That doesn't mean he was covering anything up. Could have just been sloppy police work."

"Maybe." Eliza wasn't convinced. "But I can't go to him with this. Not yet."

James sighed heavily. "What do you need from me?"

"Access to the county records. There might be connections I'm missing—property records, business dealings, anything that might link these victims beyond Nathan."

"That's it? Just records access?"

"For now. And your discretion."

James nodded slowly. "I'll help with the records. But Eliza—be careful. If you're wrong about this, you could damage a lot of relationships. And if you're right..." He let the implication hang.

"If I'm right, then someone else might disappear this year," she finished. "I can't let that happen."

After James left, promising to secure the county records access, Eliza turned back to her board. The pattern was there, she was certain. But was she seeing the whole picture, or just the pieces that fit her emerging theory?

She pulled out her phone and checked the weather forecast. The storm Nathan had mentioned was indeed approaching—heavy rain predicted for the coming weekend, almost exactly five years after Michael Reynolds' disappearance.

As she stared at the radar image of the approaching storm system, her phone buzzed with a text message. Unknown number.

She opened it and felt her breath catch. It was a photo of her apartment door, taken from the hallway outside. Nothing threatening in the image itself—just her door, number 342, with its distinctive blue paint.

But the message was clear: someone knew where she lived. Someone was watching.

And someone knew she was looking into the pattern of disappearances that had haunted Maplewood Bay for thirty years.

Eliza saved the photo, then deleted the message. She turned back to her evidence board with renewed determination. The game had changed. She wasn't just investigating anymore.

She was being investigated in return.

Chapter 3: The Victims

The county records building smelled of paper and neglect. Located on the outskirts of Maplewood Bay, the three-story brick structure housed everything from property deeds to birth certificates dating back to the town's founding in 1842. It was the kind of place bureaucracy went to die, which made it perfect for Eliza's purposes—few visitors and fewer questions.

"You owe me for this," James muttered as he led her through the labyrinthine basement corridors. His county sheriff's badge had gotten them past the sleepy security guard without issue.

"I told Marcy at the front desk we're looking into an estate dispute."

"Thank you," Eliza said, genuinely grateful. "I know this is a lot to ask."

"More than you realize. If Wallace finds out I'm helping you pursue an unauthorized investigation, especially one involving the town's most respected psychologist..."

"He won't find out," Eliza assured him. "And this isn't an investigation yet. Just... background research."

James gave her a skeptical look as he unlocked a heavy metal door marked "Archives: 1980-2000."

"Background research with a conspiracy board in the basement," he said. "Right."

The room beyond was cavernous, filled with row upon row of metal shelving units sagging under the weight of cardboard boxes and leather-bound ledgers. Dust motes danced in the shafts of light from high, narrow windows.

"Property records are in Section C," James said. "Tax assessments in D. Business licenses in F. I'll be outside keeping watch. You have two hours before I need to get back to the station."

After he left, Eliza moved methodically through the sections, pulling records related to each victim. She started with property transactions, looking for any unusual patterns around the times of the disappearances.

Three hours later—James had reluctantly extended her time—she had filled a legal pad with notes and her mind with troubling connections.

Katherine Winters, the real estate agent who disappeared in 1997, had been handling the initial property acquisitions for what would later become the Maplewood Bay Marina Redevelopment Project. According to a small article in the business section of the local paper, she had expressed "concerns about the valuation process" just weeks before she vanished.

Thomas Reeves, the teacher who disappeared in 1992, had been researching local history for a book. His notes, copied and filed with his missing persons report, mentioned "irregularities in the town council minutes from 1985-1990" regarding land use designations.

Daniel Foster, the accountant who vanished in 2002, had worked for several prominent town businesses, including the construction company that later won the bid for the marina project.

And Michael Reynolds, the journalist who disappeared in 2012, had been writing a series on the "Hidden History of Maplewood Bay," with a focus on development projects and environmental impacts.

The connections were there, but still circumstantial. What Eliza needed was something concrete—something that tied these victims together beyond their apparent interest in town business dealings.

She was about to give up when she spotted a thin folder labeled "Coastal Environmental Survey, 1985." It was misfiled in a box of business licenses, and she might have missed it entirely if not for the date—two years before the first disappearance.

Inside was a report commissioned by the county environmental office, evaluating potential contamination along the Maplewood Bay coastline. Most of it was technical jargon about water quality and soil samples, but a section near the end caught her eye:

"Area 7 (coordinates 44.32N, 123.15W) shows concerning levels of industrial chemicals consistent with illegal dumping practices. Recommend immediate containment and remediation before development of adjacent properties."

A handwritten note in the margin read: "Report suppressed by order of Mayor's Office. No further action. - J.W."

J.W. James Wallace—now Chief Wallace, but then a patrol officer with political ambitions.

Eliza's pulse quickened. She flipped to the report's cover page to find the author: Dr. Thomas Morgan, Environmental Consultant.

Her father.

She sat back, stunned. Her father had authored this report two years before Melissa Canning disappeared. A report that had been suppressed. A report about toxic contamination in an area that would later become...

She checked the coordinates against a map in the front of the folder. Area 7 was exactly where the marina development now stood.

The pieces were starting to fit together, forming a picture more disturbing than she had imagined. Not just a serial predator, but something bigger—a conspiracy involving the town's most powerful figures, spanning decades.

And her father had known something about it.

"Ms. Lindstrom? I'm Detective Morgan with the Maplewood Bay Police." Eliza showed her badge to the elderly woman who answered the door of the small bungalow on Spruce Street. "I was hoping to ask you some questions about your daughter, Sarah."

Martha Lindstrom's face showed the permanent markers of grief—lines etched by years of uncertainty and loss. Sarah Lindstrom, the librarian, had disappeared in 2007, leaving her mother in a state of suspended mourning.

"The police haven't asked about Sarah in years," Martha said, but stepped aside to let Eliza in. "Have you found something new?"

"I'm reviewing several cold cases," Eliza said carefully. "Sometimes fresh eyes notice things that were missed."

The living room was a shrine to the missing woman. Photos covered every surface—Sarah graduating college, Sarah at the beach, Sarah behind the reference desk at the Maplewood Bay Library. In each image, she wore the same warm smile, her eyes bright behind tortoiseshell glasses.

"She would be forty-one now," Martha said, following Eliza's gaze to the photos. "I still buy her birthday presents every year. Silly, isn't it?"

"Not at all," Eliza said gently. "Mrs. Lindstrom, in reviewing Sarah's case, I noticed something that wasn't fully explored in the original investigation. Did Sarah ever mention concerns about her work at the library? Any research she was doing that troubled her?"

Martha's eyes narrowed slightly. "Why do you ask that specifically?"

"Just following up on some notes in the file," Eliza said, the lie coming easily in service of the greater truth she was pursuing.

Martha was silent for a moment, then walked to a small secretary desk in the corner. She unlocked a drawer and removed a leather-bound journal.

"The police took most of Sarah's things," she said. "But they missed this. It was in her bedside table at my house—she was staying with me that week because her apartment was being painted."

She handed the journal to Eliza. "She wrote about being excited about some historical documents she'd found in the library archives. Something about land deals and environmental reports that had been 'misplaced.' She said she was going to talk to Dr. Wells about it, get his advice on what to do."

"Dr. Nathan Wells?" Eliza kept her voice neutral.

"Yes. Sarah had been seeing him for anxiety. She trusted him." Martha's voice broke slightly. "The night she disappeared, she had an appointment with him. The police confirmed she made it to the appointment, but no one saw her after that. Her car was found at the grocery store the next morning."

"With a small glass bird beside it," Eliza murmured.

Martha looked up sharply. "Yes. How did you know that detail? It wasn't in the newspaper."

"It was in the police report," Eliza said. "Mrs. Lindstrom, may I borrow this journal? I promise to return it."

"If it helps find out what happened to my daughter, you can keep it." Martha clutched Eliza's hand. "Detective, do you think after all this time, we might finally get answers?"

Eliza thought of the six victims, the pattern of disappearances, the environmental report, and the powerful men who might have wanted it all buried.

"I'm going to do everything I can," she promised.

Back in her car, Eliza called James.

"I need everything we have on my father's accident," she said when he answered.

"Your father? What does he have to do with this?"

"I found a report he wrote in 1985 about toxic contamination at what's now the marina development. The report was suppressed by the mayor's office, with Wallace's involvement."

A long silence. Then: "Eliza, be careful where you're going with this."

"I need the accident report, James. The complete file."

Another pause. "Come by my place tonight. Not the station."

After hanging up, Eliza opened Sarah Lindstrom's journal and began reading. Most entries were mundane—daily activities, complaints about coworkers, notes about books she'd enjoyed. But about two weeks before her disappearance, the entries changed:

May 14, 2007: Found something strange today while digitizing the old town records. Environmental report from 1985 that was supposed to be destroyed. Shows dangerous

39

contamination at the marina site. Report signed by someone named Morgan. Checking if there's a connection to Detective Morgan who died a few years ago.

May 18, 2007: Mentioned the report to Dr. Wells today. He seemed very interested, asked a lot of questions about who else knew about it. Suggested I bring it to our next session so he could help me decide what to do. Feel nervous about this for some reason.

May 20, 2007: Called the county environmental office about the report. The clerk got weird when I mentioned it, said all copies were supposed to have been collected years ago. When I asked why, she hung up. Definitely taking this to Dr. Wells on Thursday. This feels important.

The final entry was dated August 10, 2007—the day Sarah disappeared:

Meeting with Dr. Wells tonight. Bringing the report and my notes. Not sure who to trust anymore. If anything happens to me, look for the blue folder in the library archive, bottom drawer of the map cabinet. I made copies.

Eliza's hands trembled as she closed the journal. Sarah Lindstrom had found a copy of her father's report. She had told Nathan about it. And then she had vanished.

The blue folder. She needed to find it, if it still existed after ten years.

Her phone buzzed with a text. Unknown number again.

This time, the photo showed the interior of her apartment—her living room, taken from the doorway. Nothing disturbed or threatening, just the clear message: we can get to you anywhere.

As she stared at the image, another text came through. This one from Nathan:

Your mother and I are concerned about you. Dinner tonight? We need to talk.

Eliza's throat went dry. She typed back: Can't tonight. Working late.

His response came immediately: Tomorrow then. No excuses. Your mother is worried sick.

She didn't reply, instead starting her car and pulling away from Martha Lindstrom's house. She needed to get to the library before it closed. She needed to find that blue folder.

And she needed to be very, very careful about who knew what she was doing.

Because someone was watching. Someone knew she was getting close to the truth.

And if the pattern held, they wouldn't hesitate to make her disappear too.

The Maplewood Bay Public Library was housed in a grand Victorian building that had once been a shipping magnate's mansion. Its ornate architecture and sprawling layout made it a labyrinth of reading rooms, study carrels, and archive spaces.

Eliza badged her way past the front desk, claiming a routine follow-up on a theft report from the previous month. The reference librarian, a young man with a hipster beard and thick-framed glasses, barely glanced at her ID.

"Archives are in the basement," he said when she asked. "Map cabinet would be in the local history section, back corner. Need me to show you?"

"I'll find it," Eliza assured him.

The basement was cool and quiet, smelling of old paper and the faint mustiness that seemed endemic to library archives everywhere. Motion-sensor lights clicked on as she moved through the stacks, illuminating row after row of shelving.

The local history section was exactly where the librarian had said, and the map cabinet—a massive metal behemoth with dozens of wide, shallow drawers—dominated the back wall.

Eliza worked methodically from the bottom drawer up, careful to leave everything as she found it. In the third drawer from the bottom, tucked beneath a large topographical map of the county, she found it—a blue folder, thin with age, its edges curling slightly.

Inside was a photocopy of her father's environmental report, identical to the one she'd found in the county records building. But Sarah Lindstrom had added her own notes, meticulously documenting connections between the contaminated area, the marina development, and the people who stood to profit from it.

Names jumped out at Eliza: Mayor Richard Whitaker. Police Chief James Wallace. Construction magnate Henry Foster—Daniel Foster's father. And on the board of directors for the development corporation: Dr. Nathan Wells.

A sticky note on the last page read: "Follow the money. Property values quadrupled after environmental concerns 'resolved.' No actual remediation ever done?"

Eliza carefully photographed each page with her phone, then replaced the folder exactly as she'd found it. As she turned to leave, the lights in the archive suddenly went out.

The motion sensors should have kept them on as long as she was moving. Someone had manually cut the power.

She froze, listening. In the darkness, she could hear the soft sound of footsteps on the stairs leading to the basement.

Eliza drew her service weapon and moved silently behind a tall shelving unit, using her phone's screen to navigate. The footsteps grew closer, accompanied by the beam of a flashlight sweeping across the archive floor.

"Hello?" called a voice. "Anyone down here? We're having an electrical issue, need to clear the building."

The voice belonged to the reference librarian, but something in his tone set off warning bells. He hadn't seemed concerned about any electrical issues when she arrived, and the timing was too convenient.

Eliza remained silent, watching as the flashlight beam moved methodically through the stacks, eventually reaching the map cabinet. The librarian went straight to the third drawer from the bottom, opened it, and removed the blue folder.

So he knew exactly what she had come for. Which meant someone had told him. Which meant someone was watching her movements very closely.

The librarian tucked the folder into his jacket and turned to leave. Eliza waited until he reached the stairs, then followed at a distance, keeping to the shadows.

At the top of the stairs, she paused. The main floor of the library was dark as well, but she could see flashlight beams moving near the entrance. Multiple people. This wasn't just the librarian acting alone.

Eliza remembered the building's layout from previous visits. There was a staff exit near the children's section, on the opposite side from the main entrance. If she could reach it without being seen...

She moved carefully through the darkened library, using bookshelves for cover. As she neared the children's section, she heard voices from the main entrance.

"Did you find it?" A man's voice, familiar but not immediately identifiable.

"Yes, sir. Right where she said it would be." The librarian.

"And the detective?"

"Still down there, as far as I know. Lights are out, so she'll have to use the main stairs to exit."

"Good. Wait for her. Remember, no confrontation. Just see where she goes next."

Eliza's mind raced. They were waiting for her, planning to follow her. Which meant they didn't know how much she'd already discovered. She still had an advantage—if she could get out unseen.

The staff door was locked with a keypad. Eliza had noticed the children's librarian entering the code once during a previous visit, and her perfect memory supplied the numbers: 1-9-4-2, the year the library was established.

She entered the code and slipped outside into the rainy evening. Instead of heading to her car in the main lot, she circled around to the street behind the library and called a rideshare from her phone.

As she waited in the shadow of a large oak tree, she watched the library's main entrance. Three men emerged—the reference librarian, a uniformed security guard she didn't recognize, and a third man whose face was obscured by an umbrella. The third man was tall with the straight-backed posture of someone with military or law enforcement training.

Like Chief Wallace. Or Nathan Wells.

The rideshare arrived, and Eliza ducked into the back seat, giving the driver an address three blocks from her apartment building. She wasn't going home tonight—not when someone had already been inside her apartment.

Instead, she directed the driver to a small motel on the outskirts of town, the kind of place that accepted cash and didn't ask questions.

As the car pulled away from the curb, Eliza's phone buzzed with another text from Nathan:

Your mother is very upset that you're avoiding us. Whatever you're going through, we can help. Family dinner tomorrow night. No excuses.

Attached was a photo of her mother, smiling beside Nathan on their back porch.

It wasn't a threat—not explicitly. But the timing, coming just minutes after her narrow escape from the library, sent a clear message: We know what you're doing. We're watching. And we can get to the people you love.

Eliza turned off her phone's location services and settled back into the seat, clutching her service weapon in her pocket. The game had escalated. She was no longer just investigating cold cases.

She was now in a dangerous dance with people who had been hiding their secrets for thirty years. People who wouldn't hesitate to add her name to the list of Maplewood Bay's missing.

And she still didn't know who she could trust.

Chapter 4: The Warning

The Seaside Motel had seen better days. Paint peeled from the exterior walls, and the neon vacancy sign flickered erratically in the growing darkness. But it offered two things Eliza desperately needed: anonymity and a clear view of all approaches.

Room 17 was on the second floor, corner unit. Eliza paid cash for three nights, using the cover story of a marital spat—she needed space from her husband. The desk clerk, a weathered woman in her sixties, had barely looked up from her romance novel, just pushed the registration card and key across the counter with a disinterested "No parties, no smoking."

Now, sitting on the edge of the sagging mattress, Eliza spread the contents of her go-bag across the faded bedspread. She always kept an emergency kit in her trunk—a habit her father had instilled in her. Change of clothes, toiletries, first aid supplies, prepaid burner phone, and $500 in cash. The paranoia that had seemed excessive yesterday felt like prudent preparation today.

She powered up the burner phone and called James.

"Where are you?" he answered immediately. "I've been trying to reach you for hours."

"I had to go dark for a while," she said. "Someone's watching me, James. They were waiting for me at the library."

"Jesus, Eliza. Are you safe?"

"For now. Did you get my father's accident file?"

A pause. "Yes. And Eliza... it's not good."

Her stomach tightened. "Tell me."

"The official report says he lost control on a rainy night, went off Cliffside Road into the bay. But there are inconsistencies. The brake line damage was noted but dismissed as resulting from the impact. There was a toxicology report showing a blood alcohol level of 0.14, but your father didn't drink."

"He was a recovering alcoholic," Eliza said quietly. "Fifteen years sober when he died."

"Exactly. And here's the kicker—the responding officer was Wallace. He signed off on the accident ruling personally, bypassing the standard review process."

Eliza closed her eyes, absorbing the implications. "They killed him, James. Because of what he knew about the contamination."

"It's possible," James admitted. "But Eliza, this goes beyond Nathan Wells. If what you're suggesting is true, this involves the highest levels of town leadership spanning decades."

"I know. I found Sarah Lindstrom's research at the library. She connected my father's environmental report to the marina development project. Nathan was on the board of directors."

"Was?"

"Still is. The development corporation continues to manage the property and is behind the current expansion project."

James was silent for a moment. "You need to bring this to Internal Affairs. Or the State Police."

"With what evidence? Circumstantial connections and a thirty-year-old environmental report? They'd shut me down before I could finish explaining." Eliza ran a hand through her hair. "I need something concrete. Something that proves the disappearances are connected to the cover-up."

"And how exactly do you plan to get that?"

"I'm working on it." She hesitated. "James, there's something else. Nathan texted me. He's insisting I come to dinner tomorrow night. Says my mother is worried."

"Are you going to go?"

"I don't see how I can avoid it without raising more suspicion. But I don't like the idea of sitting across the table from him, knowing what I know now."

"Maybe you should stay away from both of them until we figure this out."

"And confirm his suspicions that I'm onto him? Besides, my mother could be in danger if he thinks I've told her anything."

James sighed heavily. "I don't like any of this, Eliza. You're in over your head."

"I know. But I can't stop now." She glanced at the motel room door, double-checking the chain lock. "I need you to do something for me. Check if there have been any recent inquiries about environmental testing at the marina. With the expansion project underway, they might have had to file new permits."

"I'll see what I can find. Where are you staying?"

"Better if you don't know. I'll contact you tomorrow." She paused. "And James? Be careful who you talk to about this."

After hanging up, Eliza laid back on the bed, staring at the water-stained ceiling. The pieces were coming together, forming a picture more disturbing than she had initially imagined. Not just a serial predator, but a conspiracy to silence anyone who threatened to expose the truth about the contamination and the powerful people who had covered it up.

Her father had discovered it. Others had stumbled upon pieces of the puzzle over the years. And one by one, they had disappeared.

The five-year pattern suddenly made more sense—it wasn't about a killer's compulsion, but about maintaining the secret whenever someone got too close. And with the marina expansion project now underway, the stakes were higher than ever.

Eliza's phone—her regular one—buzzed with a text from her mother: Honey, please call me. Nathan says you're avoiding us. I'm worried about you.

She typed back: Sorry, busy with a case. Will come for dinner tomorrow night. Love you.

Then she turned off the phone completely. She needed to think, to plan her next move carefully.

Because tomorrow night, she would be sitting across the table from a man who might have been involved in multiple disappearances—including orchestrating her own father's death.

And she needed to be ready.

The evidence wall in the basement storage room had been destroyed.

Eliza stood in the doorway, surveying the damage. The corkboard had been torn from the wall, photos and documents scattered across the floor, many of them shredded. Red string lay in tangled heaps like spilled blood.

"What the hell happened?" James appeared behind her, his expression darkening as he took in the scene.

"Someone doesn't appreciate my interior decorating," Eliza said, keeping her voice steady despite the rage building inside her. She knelt to examine a torn photograph—Melissa Canning's smiling face, ripped in half.

"This had to be someone with access to the building," James said. "I'll check the security logs."

"Don't bother. They'll have covered their tracks." Eliza picked up a crumpled piece of paper, smoothing it out. It was a note, typed on plain white paper: Some secrets stay buried.

She handed it to James, who read it with a deepening frown. "This is a direct threat, Eliza. We need to report this."

"To who? Wallace? The same man who covered up my father's murder?" She shook her head. "This just confirms I'm on the right track."

"Or it confirms you're in serious danger." James ran a hand through his hair. "Look, I checked into those environmental permits like you asked. The marina expansion required new testing, but the results are being kept confidential under some obscure municipal code. I'd need a court order to access them."

"Which we won't get without evidence of wrongdoing," Eliza finished. "It's a perfect circle."

She began gathering the scattered documents, salvaging what she could. Most of her evidence was backed up—photos on her phone, notes in her apartment—but the destruction of the wall was a message. Someone wanted her to know they could reach her anywhere, even in the secure areas of the police station.

"Did you find anything else?" she asked James.

"Maybe. I looked into property transfers around the times of the disappearances, like you suggested. There's a pattern—in each case, property values in the marina district jumped significantly within months after the person vanished. It's as if their disappearance removed an obstacle to development or expansion."

"Or removed someone who knew too much," Eliza added.

"Exactly. And there's something else." James lowered his voice, though they were alone in the basement. "I found a connection to your father's accident. The week before he died, he had requested access to the original environmental samples from the 1985 survey. The request was denied by the mayor's office."

Eliza's throat tightened. "He was going back to prove the contamination was still there."

"Looks that way. And Eliza—the current expansion project includes plans for a residential complex. Luxury condos built directly over what your father identified as the most contaminated area."

The implications were staggering. If the contamination had never been properly remediated, as Sarah Lindstrom had suspected, then the development could expose hundreds of people to toxic chemicals. The liability would be enormous—enough to destroy the fortunes and reputations of everyone involved in the original cover-up.

"When does construction start on the residential phase?" she asked.

"Groundbreaking ceremony is next week. Mayor Whitaker and the development board are all scheduled to attend. Including Dr. Wells."

Eliza checked her watch. Four hours until dinner at her mother's house. Four hours to prepare to face Nathan.

"I need to get into Nathan's office," she said suddenly.

"His office? Are you insane?"

"He keeps patient files there. If he's connected to the victims, there might be records."

"That's completely illegal, not to mention dangerous. Patient files are confidential, and breaking into his office would end your career if you're caught."

"I'm not talking about breaking in." Eliza's mind was racing ahead. "My mother has a key. Nathan gave it to her in case of emergencies. She keeps it in her kitchen drawer."

James stared at her. "You're going to steal the key from your mother?"

"Borrow," Eliza corrected. "Just long enough to make a copy."

"This is crossing a line, Eliza."

"The line was crossed when six people disappeared and my father was murdered." Her voice was steel. "Are you with me or not?"

James was silent for a long moment. "What do you need me to do?"

"Cover for me tonight. If anyone asks, we're working the Westside burglaries together."

"And if you find something in his office?"

"Then we take it to the State Police. With enough evidence, they can't ignore us."

James nodded reluctantly. "Be careful tonight. If Nathan suspects what you know..."

"He won't," Eliza assured him, with more confidence than she felt. "I've been underestimating him for years. Now it's his turn to underestimate me."

Patricia Morgan's house glowed warmly in the evening light, a picture of domestic tranquility that belied the tension Eliza felt as she approached the front door. She had changed clothes at the motel, opting for a casual sweater and jeans that concealed her service weapon in a back holster.

Her mother answered the door with a relieved smile. "There you are! We were starting to worry."

"Sorry, work's been crazy." Eliza accepted her mother's hug, breathing in the familiar scent of gardenia perfume. Over her mother's shoulder, she saw Nathan in the kitchen doorway, watching them with an unreadable expression.

"Eliza," he greeted her. "Glad you could join us after all."

Was there a subtle emphasis on "after all"? A hint that he knew she'd been avoiding them? Eliza forced a smile.

"Wouldn't miss Mom's cooking," she said lightly.

Dinner was an exercise in controlled tension. Patricia chatted about wedding plans and neighborhood gossip, seemingly oblivious to the undercurrents between her daughter and fiancé. Nathan was the perfect host—attentive, charming, asking Eliza about her work with what appeared to be genuine interest.

"Your mother mentioned you've been reviewing cold cases," he said as they moved to coffee and dessert. "Anything interesting?"

Eliza met his gaze steadily. "Some patterns that were overlooked. It's amazing what you can find when you look at the big picture instead of isolated incidents."

"Patterns are fascinating psychological phenomena," Nathan nodded. "Our brains are wired to find them, even when they might not exist. It's called apophenia—the tendency to perceive connections between unrelated events."

"These connections are quite real," Eliza said, maintaining her composure. "Just overlooked."

"Well, I hope you're being careful," her mother interjected. "Some of those old cases can be disturbing."

"I'm always careful, Mom." Eliza smiled reassuringly. "Actually, could I get some water? My throat's a bit dry."

"Of course, honey. Nathan, would you mind getting the pitcher from the refrigerator? I need to check on the pie."

As both of them left the dining room, Eliza moved quickly to the kitchen drawer where her mother kept spare keys. She found Nathan's office key exactly where she remembered, slipped it into her pocket, and was back in her seat before either of them returned.

"So, Nathan," she said when they were all seated again, "how's the marina development project coming along? Mom mentioned you're on the board."

If the question surprised him, he didn't show it. "Moving forward nicely. The expansion will bring significant economic benefits to Maplewood Bay."

"I heard there are plans for residential units," Eliza pressed. "Any environmental concerns with building on that site? I seem to recall there were issues years ago."

A flicker of something—surprise? wariness?—crossed Nathan's face before his professional mask returned. "All necessary testing has been done. The site is perfectly safe."

"That's good to hear. Wasn't there an environmental report back in the eighties that found contamination there?"

Patricia looked confused. "What an odd question, Eliza. Why would you ask about that?"

But Nathan's eyes had narrowed slightly. "There was a preliminary report, yes. But subsequent testing showed the initial findings were flawed. The scientist who conducted the original survey had... methodological issues."

"The scientist," Eliza repeated. "You mean Dr. Thomas Morgan? My father?"

A heavy silence fell over the table. Patricia looked between them, bewildered. "Thomas did environmental work before joining the police, but I don't remember anything about the marina."

"It was a minor project," Nathan said smoothly. "And as I said, his findings were later disproven."

"By whom?" Eliza asked.

"Eliza, what's this about?" her mother interrupted. "Why are you interrogating Nathan about some old report?"

"Just curious, Mom. Professional interest." Eliza forced a smile. "Sorry if it seemed like an interrogation."

Nathan studied her for a long moment. "Your father was a good man, Eliza. But like all of us, he made mistakes. His environmental work wasn't his strength—that's why he changed careers."

The implication that her father had been incompetent made Eliza's blood boil, but she maintained her composure. "He seemed to think the contamination was significant. Significant enough to request follow-up testing the week before he died."

Patricia gasped softly. "Eliza! What are you saying?"

Nathan's expression hardened almost imperceptibly. "I think you're confused. Thomas's accident was a tragedy, but it had nothing to do with his former work."

"The accident," Eliza echoed. "You mean when his brake lines were cut and his toxicology report was falsified to show alcohol in his system despite fifteen years of sobriety?"

"Eliza!" Her mother's face had gone pale. "Stop this right now!"

Nathan placed a calming hand on Patricia's arm. "It's alright, Patricia. Eliza is obviously working through some issues with her father's death. It's not uncommon for children to create alternative narratives when dealing with traumatic loss." He turned to Eliza, his voice taking on the professional tone he used with patients. "Have you been sleeping well, Eliza? Stress and sleep deprivation can trigger paranoid ideation."

The clinical assessment—the subtle suggestion that she was becoming unstable—was exactly the response Eliza had expected. Nathan was too skilled to react defensively. Instead, he was positioning her as the troubled one, using his professional authority to undermine her credibility.

"I'm sleeping fine," she said evenly. "And my ideation is based on evidence, not paranoia."

"What evidence?" her mother demanded. "Eliza, you're talking about your father's death as if... as if it wasn't an accident."

"I'm just asking questions, Mom." Eliza softened her tone. "Questions about why an environmental report was suppressed. Why property values skyrocketed after contamination concerns mysteriously disappeared. Why six people who asked similar questions over the years have vanished without a trace."

Nathan's expression remained neutral, but Eliza saw his hand tighten slightly around his coffee cup. "Six people? What are you talking about?"

"Cold cases," Eliza said. "Spanning thirty years. All connected to the marina development in some way. All disappeared after expressing concerns or finding information they shouldn't have."

"And you think these cold cases are connected to Thomas's accident?" Nathan's tone was perfectly calibrated—concerned but skeptical, the voice of reason addressing delusion.

"I think there's a pattern that deserves investigation."

"Patterns again." Nathan shook his head sadly. "Eliza, I'm concerned about you. This fixation on connecting unrelated events, this conspiracy theory involving your father's death—these are warning signs of psychological distress."

"Don't psychoanalyze me, Nathan." Eliza's voice was steel. "I'm not one of your patients."

"No, you're family. Which is why I'm worried." He turned to Patricia. "Has she talked to you about any of this before?"

Patricia shook her head, looking distressed. "No, this is the first I'm hearing of it. Eliza, honey, maybe you should take some time off work. You've been under so much pressure lately."

The unified front was exactly what Nathan had intended—positioning Eliza as troubled and irrational, with him as the concerned professional and her mother as the worried parent. It was masterfully done.

But Eliza had anticipated this. "You're right, Mom. I have been under pressure. And maybe I'm connecting dots that aren't there." She forced a rueful smile. "Occupational hazard of detective work."

The tension in the room eased slightly. Nathan nodded approvingly. "It happens to the best of us. The mind seeks patterns, even in randomness."

"Exactly." Eliza stood. "I should go. Early shift tomorrow."

"Are you sure you're alright to drive?" her mother asked. "You could stay in your old room tonight."

"I'm fine, Mom. Really." Eliza hugged her mother tightly, whispering, "I love you," with an intensity that made Patricia pull back to look at her questioningly.

"I love you too, honey. Call me tomorrow?"

"I will." Eliza turned to Nathan, extending her hand formally. "Sorry if I upset you with my questions."

He took her hand, his grip firm. "No apology necessary. My door is always open if you want to talk more about your concerns."

The double meaning wasn't lost on Eliza. As their hands clasped, she felt something press into her palm—a small, hard object that Nathan transferred with the smoothness of a practiced magician.

She closed her fingers around it, maintaining her composure as she said her goodbyes and walked to her car. Only when she was inside with the doors locked did she open her hand to see what Nathan had given her.

A small metal bird. Identical to the ones left at the scenes of the disappearances.

It wasn't just a warning. It was a confession.

And as Eliza stared at the tiny figure gleaming in her palm, her phone rang. James's number.

"Eliza," his voice was tight with urgency. "There's been an accident. My car... the brakes failed on Cliffside Road. I'm at Maplewood General. They're saying I'm lucky to be alive."

The same road where her father had died. The same type of sabotage.

"It's not a coincidence," she whispered.

"No," James agreed grimly. "It's a message. They know we're getting close."

Eliza closed her fingers around the metal bird, her resolve hardening. "I'm coming to the hospital. Don't talk to anyone until I get there."

As she started her car, she glanced back at her mother's house. Nathan stood at the window, watching her. Even from a distance, she could feel the weight of his gaze—calculating, assessing.

The game had changed. Nathan had shown his hand, confirming her suspicions while simultaneously undermining her credibility with her mother. And now James had nearly been killed—a warning that no one close to her was safe.

Eliza pulled away from the curb, the metal bird clutched in her hand like a talisman. She had what she needed now—Nathan's office key and confirmation that he was involved. Tonight, while he was with her mother, she would find the evidence to bring him down.

Before anyone else disappeared. Before anyone else died.

Before the five-year clock ticked down to another victim.

Chapter 5: The Doubt

The fluorescent lights of Maplewood General Hospital buzzed overhead, casting a sickly glow across the institutional green walls of the fourth-floor corridor. Eliza clutched the small metal bird in her pocket as she approached Room 412, her mind racing with implications. The weight of the object—Nathan's implicit confession—felt heavier than its physical mass should allow.

James Harlow looked diminished against the white hospital sheets, his normally commanding presence reduced by bandages and the thin hospital gown. A monitor beeped steadily beside him, tracking vital signs. His right leg was elevated, encased in a cast, and a series of butterfly bandages crossed his forehead above his left eye.

"You look terrible," Eliza said, attempting lightness she didn't feel.

James managed a weak smile. "You should see the other guy. Oh wait—there wasn't one. Just a mysteriously severed brake line and a guardrail that barely stopped me from joining your father at the bottom of Cliffside Bay."

Eliza pulled a chair close to the bed, glancing at the door to ensure they were alone. "Tell me exactly what happened."

"Not much to tell. I was heading home after checking those property records you asked about. Coming down Cliffside Road, I hit the brakes for the sharp turn near Miller's Point, and the pedal went straight to the floor." His voice was matter-of-fact, but Eliza could see the lingering fear in his eyes. "If it hadn't been for the new guardrail they installed last year, we wouldn't be having this conversation."

"The same road where my father died," Eliza said quietly.

"The same method too. I had them check the car before they towed it. Brake line was cleanly cut—professional job, not a stress fracture or wear."

Eliza's hand tightened around the metal bird. "It's a message. They know we're investigating together."

"They?"

She hesitated, then pulled out the bird, placing it on the white hospital blanket between them. "Nathan gave me this tonight. Slipped it into my hand when we said goodbye. It's identical to the tokens left at each disappearance scene."

James stared at the object, his expression darkening. "That's not just a message. That's a confession."

"And a threat." Eliza recounted the dinner conversation, Nathan's subtle psychological tactics, and her mother's unwitting role in his gaslighting strategy.

"He's positioning you as unstable," James observed. "Classic abuser technique—isolate the target, undermine their credibility, make them doubt themselves."

"It's working with my mother. She thinks I'm having some kind of breakdown."

"Are you sure you're not?" The question was gentle, but direct. "Eliza, I believe you about the pattern, the disappearances, even the environmental cover-up. But we need to consider the possibility that Nathan gave you that bird for another reason—to make you appear paranoid if you accuse him."

The suggestion stung, but Eliza forced herself to consider it objectively. Was she connecting dots that weren't there? Seeing patterns where coincidence existed? The doubt crept in, unwelcome but necessary.

"I know how it sounds," she admitted. "Detective with perfect memory becomes obsessed with cold cases, creates conspiracy theory involving her mother's fiancé, claims town leaders are behind multiple disappearances."

"When you put it that way, it does sound like the plot of a bad thriller." James attempted a smile that turned into a grimace as he shifted position. "But someone cut my brake lines, Eliza. That's not in your head."

"Unless it was a random act of vandalism and the timing is coincidental."

"Do you believe that?"

She thought of the destroyed evidence wall, the threatening texts, the library ambush, and now James in the hospital. "No. There are too many connected events."

"Then trust your instincts." James reached for the call button. "I need to increase my pain meds. And you need to decide your next move."

"I already have." Eliza pocketed the bird. "Nathan's office. Tonight. While he's with my mother."

James's eyes widened. "Breaking and entering? Illegal search? That's career suicide if you're caught."

"I'm not breaking in. I have a key." She explained about copying her mother's spare. "And it's not a search—it's a wellness check on a potentially suicidal patient."

"That's thin, even for probable cause."

"I don't need probable cause if I'm not acting as a police officer." Eliza stood. "This is personal, James. Off the books."

"That's exactly what worries me." He caught her wrist. "Promise me you'll be careful. These people have already killed once—maybe multiple times."

"I'll be careful." She squeezed his hand. "Get some rest. I'll call you tomorrow."

As she turned to leave, James called after her: "Eliza. If you find something concrete, don't confront Nathan alone. Call me first, no matter what time."

She nodded, but they both knew it was a promise she might not keep.

The storm that had been threatening for days finally arrived as Eliza left the hospital, rain lashing against the windows of her car in rhythmic waves. The weather report on the radio warned of potential flooding in low-lying areas, including parts of the marina district. Perfect conditions for another disappearance, if the pattern held.

She drove to her apartment building but parked two blocks away, approaching on foot through the rain. The memory of the photo someone had sent—her living room, taken from inside her apartment—made her cautious. She entered through the service entrance, taking the stairs instead of the elevator, her hand resting on her service weapon.

Her apartment door showed no signs of tampering, but that meant nothing if her intruder had a key. She entered cautiously, clearing each room with professional efficiency before allowing herself to relax marginally.

The space felt different somehow—violated. Nothing was obviously disturbed, but Eliza sensed the lingering presence of an unwelcome visitor. She moved to the kitchen, pulling a bottle of water from the refrigerator, and noticed a small detail: the magnetic notepad on the fridge door was aligned perfectly straight. She always left it slightly askew.

Someone had been here again. Recently.

Fighting the urge to flee, Eliza forced herself to think strategically. If they wanted to harm her, they'd had ample opportunity. This was psychological warfare—letting her know she was watched, that nowhere was safe.

She moved quickly, gathering essential items: laptop, backup files, the copied key to Nathan's office, and her father's old service revolver from the lockbox in her closet. The weapon was technically illegal for her to carry—unregistered, kept for sentimental reasons—but tonight she wanted a backup that couldn't be traced through department records.

As she packed, her police radio crackled with reports of flooding near the marina. Emergency services were being deployed to assist with evacuations of the lowest-lying areas. The storm was intensifying, just as the forecast had predicted.

Five years ago, almost to the day, Michael Reynolds had disappeared during similar weather conditions.

Eliza's phone rang—her mother.

"Honey? Are you okay? The storm is getting worse, and I'm worried about you driving."

"I'm fine, Mom. At home, staying dry." The lie came easily, necessary to protect her mother from what was coming.

"Nathan's worried too. He says you seemed upset at dinner."

Eliza could picture Nathan beside her mother, listening, perhaps even prompting the call. "Just tired. Work stress."

"He thinks you should take some time off. Maybe see someone professionally."

"Someone like him, you mean?" Eliza couldn't keep the edge from her voice.

"Well, no, that would be inappropriate given our relationship. But he could recommend someone." Patricia's voice softened. "Honey, I know your father's death affected you deeply.

Sometimes trauma resurfaces years later in unexpected ways."

The manipulation was so perfect, so insidious, that Eliza almost admired its craftsmanship. Nathan was using her mother's genuine concern to further his narrative of Eliza's mental instability.

"I appreciate the concern, Mom, but I'm fine. Really." She forced warmth into her tone. "How long is Nathan staying tonight?"

"Oh, he's here for the duration, I think. This storm is too dangerous to drive in. He's working in the den now—some patient files he brought home to review."

Perfect. Nathan would be occupied for hours, giving Eliza a clear window to search his office.

"That's good. You shouldn't be alone during weather like this." Eliza meant it, though not for the reasons her mother would assume. "I love you, Mom."

"I love you too, sweetheart. Stay safe."

After hanging up, Eliza checked the time: 9:17 PM. Nathan's office was a fifteen-minute drive in good weather, longer in the storm. She needed to move quickly.

As she gathered her rain gear, her phone buzzed with a weather alert: Flash flood warning for coastal areas of Maplewood Bay, including the marina district and downtown. Residents advised to seek higher ground.

The timing was too perfect to be coincidental. If the pattern held, someone would disappear tonight—someone who threatened the secrets Nathan and his associates had kept buried for decades.

Unless Eliza found the evidence she needed to stop it.

Dr. Nathan Wells maintained his practice in a converted Victorian home on Maple Street, just off the town square. The building housed three other professionals—a dentist, an accountant, and a lawyer—but at this hour, and in this weather, the parking lot was empty.

Eliza parked two blocks away, behind the public library, and approached on foot, rain pelting her hooded figure. The storm provided perfect cover—no one would question why her face was obscured, or why she moved quickly through the deserted streets.

The building's security system was basic—a keypad at the main entrance that Eliza had memorized the code for years ago, when she occasionally met her mother there for lunch. Inside, the common areas were dimly lit by emergency lighting, the power fluctuating with the storm.

Nathan's office was on the second floor, rear corner—the most private location in the building. The door bore a simple plaque: "Dr. Nathan Wells, Ph.D. - Clinical Psychology."

Eliza's hand trembled slightly as she inserted the copied key. This was the point of no return—a line crossed that could end her career if discovered. But if she was right about Nathan, her career was the least of what she stood to lose.

The lock turned smoothly, and she slipped inside, closing the door behind her. The office was dark except for the occasional flash of lightning through the windows. She used her penlight rather than turning on the main lights, sweeping the narrow beam across the familiar space.

The outer office contained a reception desk and waiting area, tastefully decorated in soothing blues and grays. Eliza moved past it to the inner door—Nathan's consultation room.

This space she knew well from her own sessions after her father's death. The comfortable leather chairs, the discreet box of tissues, the diplomas and certifications on the wall, the bookshelf filled with psychology texts and self-help titles. It was designed to convey competence, compassion, and safety.

But Eliza wasn't interested in the consultation room. She moved to the door behind Nathan's desk—his private office, where he kept patient files and personal records.

This door required a separate key, which her mother didn't possess. Eliza removed a small lock-picking set from her pocket—a skill she'd learned during specialized training for the detective exam. It took longer than she'd hoped, her hands less steady than usual, but eventually the lock yielded.

The private office was smaller, more utilitarian. A desk with computer, filing cabinets along one wall, a small safe in the corner. Eliza started with the filing cabinets, methodically checking each drawer.

The patient files were organized alphabetically, and Eliza quickly located those for the known victims: Melissa Canning, Thomas Reeves, Katherine Winters, Daniel Foster, Sarah Lindstrom, Michael Reynolds. Each folder was surprisingly thin, containing only basic intake forms and minimal session notes.

Too minimal. As if they'd been sanitized.

She photographed each file with her phone, then turned her attention to the desk. The computer was password-protected, as expected. She could try to crack it, but that would take time she might not have.

The desk drawers contained standard office supplies, reference materials, appointment books. In the bottom drawer, she found a series of leather-bound journals—Nathan's personal notebooks, dating back decades.

Eliza selected those corresponding to the years of the disappearances and began skimming, photographing relevant pages. The entries were in Nathan's precise handwriting, often clinical in tone, discussing patients by initials rather than names.

A passage from October 1987 caught her eye:

M.C. continues to express concern about water quality samples from Area 7. Suggested her anxiety might be projection of unresolved grief over father's death. She remains fixated. Consultation with R.W. may be necessary if she pursues testing independently.

R.W.—Richard Whitaker, the mayor. And M.C.—Melissa Canning, the first victim.

Eliza's pulse quickened as she found similar entries for each victim:

May 1992: T.R. discovered historical council minutes regarding Area 7 rezoning. His "historical research" becoming problematic. Informed appropriate parties.

September 1997: K.W. expressing ethical concerns about property valuations near marina. Attempted redirection unsuccessful. Situation requires intervention.

November 2002: D.F. accessed financial records showing remediation fund misappropriation. Severe anxiety about professional obligations. Situation untenable.

August 2007: S.L. located copy of Morgan environmental report. Directly threatened project viability. Immediate action required.

October 2012: M.R. investigating historical pattern of "accidents" related to development projects. Has connected several cases. Containment impossible through conventional means.

And most recently, dated just one week ago:

E.M. showing dangerous fixation on cold cases. Pattern recognition abilities making connections others have missed. Mother reports increasing paranoia and obsessive behavior. Traditional discrediting may be insufficient given department position. Monitoring continues.

E.M. Eliza Morgan. Her own name in Nathan's journal of victims.

The confirmation was both vindicating and terrifying. Nathan wasn't just aware of the disappearances—he had documented his role in identifying targets who threatened to expose the environmental cover-up.

But the journals didn't explicitly confirm he had caused the disappearances, only that he had identified the threats and consulted with "appropriate parties." There had to be more.

Eliza turned her attention to the safe. A small, wall-mounted model with a digital keypad. She could try to crack it, but that would take specialized equipment she didn't have.

Instead, she studied it carefully, looking for clues. Nathan was methodical, a creature of habit. He would use a meaningful number sequence, something he could remember without writing down.

She thought about what she knew of him. His birthday: 04-17-1952. His license number: 78342. The address of his first practice: 1224 Elm Street.

None seemed right. Then she remembered something her mother had mentioned once—Nathan's cabin in the mountains, his private retreat. The address was 4075 Pinecrest Road.

Eliza tried the sequence: 4-0-7-5.

The safe remained locked.

She tried again, reversing it: 5-7-0-4.

Nothing.

Then she had another thought. The pattern of disappearances—every five years, starting in 1987.

She entered: 1-9-8-7.

The safe beeped and the door swung open.

Inside was a single USB drive and a small wooden box. Eliza took both, her hands trembling slightly. The box contained six small objects—bird figurines identical to the one Nathan had given her, each tagged with initials and dates corresponding to the disappearances.

Trophies. Like a serial killer would keep.

The USB drive would have to wait until she had access to a secure computer. She pocketed both items and carefully closed the safe, making sure to leave everything else exactly as she had found it.

As she prepared to leave, a flash of lightning illuminated the room, drawing her attention to something she had missed—a framed photograph on the wall behind the door. It showed a group of men standing in front of a rustic cabin. Eliza recognized Nathan, Mayor Whitaker, Chief Wallace, and several other prominent town figures.

And standing slightly apart from the group, looking uncomfortable, was her father.

The photo was dated July 1985—two months before her father's environmental report was filed.

Eliza photographed it, then made her final preparations to leave. She had what she needed now—evidence linking Nathan to the disappearances, proof of the conspiracy involving town leadership, and confirmation that her father had been murdered for what he knew.

As she carefully locked the office door behind her, her phone vibrated. A text from an unknown number:

Journalist Carey Bennett missing. Car found at marina parking lot. Thought you should know.

Carey Bennett—the reporter who had been investigating the marina expansion project. The next victim, right on schedule.

The five-year clock had chimed again.

The storm had intensified, rain coming down in blinding sheets as Eliza made her way back to her car. The streets were beginning to flood, water pooling at intersections and flowing along gutters with increasing force.

Emergency vehicle sirens wailed in the distance, heading toward the marina district where the flooding was worst. And where Carey Bennett's car had been found.

Eliza started her engine, then hesitated. Going to the marina now would be expected—the obvious move of a detective responding to a missing person report. If Nathan or his associates were watching, that's where they'd expect to find her.

But Nathan wasn't at the marina. He was at her mother's house.

The realization hit her with sudden clarity. She had been so focused on finding evidence that she hadn't considered the most obvious threat: her mother was alone with a man who had been involved in multiple disappearances.

Patricia Morgan wasn't a threat to the conspiracy—she knew nothing about the environmental cover-up or her late husband's role in discovering it. But she was important to Eliza. The perfect leverage.

Eliza pulled away from the curb, tires splashing through deepening puddles as she headed not toward the marina, but toward her mother's house on the other side of town. The normally fifteen-minute drive took nearly thirty in the storm conditions, each minute stretching her nerves tighter.

As she approached the familiar street, she cut her headlights and parked a block away, approaching on foot through neighbors' yards to avoid being seen from the road.

Her mother's house was lit up against the darkness, warm light spilling from windows onto the rain-soaked lawn. Through the living room window, Eliza could see Patricia sitting in her favorite armchair, reading glasses perched on her nose as she paged through a magazine. Alone.

Where was Nathan?

Eliza circled the house cautiously, checking each window. The kitchen was empty, as was the dining room. The den light was on, but she couldn't see inside from her angle.

She moved to the back of the house, where a small covered porch offered some shelter from the rain. The back door was locked, but Eliza still had her key. She entered quietly, water dripping from her rain jacket onto the mudroom floor.

"Mom?" she called softly, not wanting to startle Patricia.

No answer.

Eliza moved through the kitchen toward the living room, hand resting on her service weapon. "Mom? It's Eliza."

Patricia looked up from her magazine, startled. "Eliza! What on earth are you doing here in this weather? And why are you soaking wet?"

"Where's Nathan?" Eliza asked, scanning the room.

"He left about an hour ago. Emergency with a patient." Patricia set aside her reading. "Honey, what's wrong? You look terrible."

"Did he say which patient? Where he was going?"

"No, just that it was urgent. He seemed quite concerned." Patricia stood, moving toward her daughter. "Eliza, you're scaring me. What's happening?"

Eliza's mind raced. Nathan had left an hour ago—right around when Carey Bennett was reported missing. The timing couldn't be coincidental.

"Mom, I need you to come with me. Right now. Pack a bag, just essentials."

"What? Why would I—"

"Please, Mom. I can't explain everything right now, but you're not safe here."

Patricia's expression shifted from confusion to concern. "Is this about what you were saying at dinner? About Nathan and your father's accident? Honey, I think you need help."

"What I need is for you to trust me." Eliza took her mother's hands. "Have I ever given you reason to doubt my judgment? My sanity?"

"No, but—"

"Then trust me now. Please."

Something in Eliza's tone must have conveyed the urgency, because Patricia nodded slowly. "Alright. Give me five minutes to pack a few things."

While her mother gathered essentials, Eliza called James at the hospital.

"Nathan's gone," she said when he answered. "Left my mother's house about an hour ago, claimed it was a patient emergency. And Carey Bennett is missing—car found at the marina."

"Jesus," James breathed. "Did you find anything at his office?"

"Everything. Patient files on all the victims, journals documenting his role in identifying them as threats, even trophies—bird figurines for each victim."

"That's enough for an arrest warrant."

"Not without explaining how I obtained it. And not in time to help Carey Bennett, if she's still alive." Eliza watched her mother moving around the bedroom, gathering clothes. "I'm taking my mother somewhere safe, then I'm going to the marina."

"The marina's flooding, Eliza. Emergency services are evacuating the area."

"Exactly. It's chaos down there—perfect conditions for making someone disappear. Or for finding someone who doesn't want to be found."

"You think Nathan took Bennett to the marina? In a flood?"

"I think the marina is where all of this started—with my father's environmental report about toxic contamination. It's where the evidence is buried, literally and figuratively."

"You can't go alone. I'm checking myself out."

"With a broken leg and concussion? No, you're staying put." Eliza's tone brooked no argument. "I'll call for backup if I find anything."

"Promise me, Eliza. No heroics."

"I promise." Another necessary lie. "I'll call you when my mother's secure."

After hanging up, Eliza helped Patricia finish packing, then ushered her to the car parked down the street. The rain had somehow intensified further, visibility reduced to just a few feet ahead of their headlights.

"Where are we going?" Patricia asked as they pulled away from the curb.

"Somewhere safe." Eliza had already decided—the Pinecrest Motel on the edge of town, a place Nathan wouldn't think to look. "I need to drop you off, then handle something for work."

"In this weather? Eliza, whatever it is can wait until morning."

"No, Mom. It can't." Eliza navigated carefully through flooded streets. "Someone's life depends on it."

Patricia fell silent, studying her daughter's profile in the dim light. After a moment, she asked quietly, "This is about Nathan, isn't it? You really believe he's involved in something terrible."

"I don't believe it, Mom. I know it." Eliza kept her eyes on the road. "I found evidence tonight. Solid evidence."

"Of what, exactly?"

How much to tell her? Patricia deserved the truth, but the full truth might be too devastating, too dangerous.

"Nathan has been identifying people who discovered information about environmental contamination at the marina site. People who later disappeared." Eliza chose her words carefully. "Including Dad."

Patricia's sharp intake of breath was audible even over the storm. "Your father's accident... you're saying it wasn't an accident?"

"His brake lines were cut. The toxicology report was falsified to show alcohol in his system."

"How do you know this?"

"I've been investigating cold cases. Six disappearances over thirty years, all connected to the marina development. All people who found information about toxic contamination that was covered up. Dad was working on an environmental report just before he died."

Patricia was silent for a long moment. "And you think Nathan is responsible? For all of this?"

"He's part of it. There are others—Mayor Whitaker, Chief Wallace, other town leaders. They've been covering up the contamination for decades. Anyone who threatened to expose it disappeared."

"This is... it's unbelievable, Eliza."

"I know how it sounds. But I have evidence, Mom. Nathan kept records. Trophies."

They had reached the Pinecrest Motel, its neon vacancy sign flickering in the storm. Eliza parked near the office.

"I need you to stay here, under a false name. Don't call anyone, don't tell anyone where you are." She handed her mother cash for the room. "I'll come back as soon as I can."

"Where are you going?"

"To the marina. There's another victim—a journalist who was investigating the expansion project. She disappeared tonight."

Patricia grabbed her arm. "Eliza, if what you're saying is true, it's too dangerous. These people have killed before."

"That's why I have to go. Before they kill again." Eliza hugged her mother tightly. "I love you, Mom. Trust me, please."

Patricia's eyes filled with tears. "I do trust you. But I'm terrified for you."

"I'll be careful." Eliza helped her mother to the motel office, waited until she had secured a room, then returned to her car.

As she pulled back onto the flooded road, heading toward the marina district, her phone buzzed with a text. Unknown number again:

She's not the only one in danger tonight. Check Nathan's beach house. Hurry.

The beach house—Nathan's weekend property on the north shore, isolated and private. The perfect place to take someone you didn't want found.

Eliza changed course, tires splashing through deepening water as she headed north, toward the coast, toward Nathan's beach house.

Toward what she increasingly feared would be a confrontation with the man who had orchestrated her father's death and the disappearances of six others.

The man who, until recently, she had trusted as a father figure.

The man who now knew she had discovered his secrets.

The storm raged around her, wind and rain lashing at her car as if nature itself was trying to prevent her from reaching her destination. But Eliza pressed on, driven by a determination that transcended fear.

She had spent her life trusting her perfect memory, believing that what she saw and recorded was objective truth. But now, for the first time, doubt crept in. Not about the evidence—that was irrefutable. But about her ability to face what waited at the end of this storm-lashed road.

Because the hardest truth wasn't that Nathan was a monster. It was that she had never seen it, despite all the signs that must have been there.

Her perfect memory had failed her in the most fundamental way.

And that doubt—that crack in her certainty—was more terrifying than any storm.

Chapter 6: The Connection

Nathan Wells' beach house perched on the northern cliffs of Maplewood Bay like a sentinel, its modern glass and cedar construction a stark contrast to the Victorian architecture that dominated the town proper. In daylight, the property offered panoramic views of the coastline. Tonight, it was barely visible through the storm, only the occasional flash of lightning revealing its silhouette against the turbulent sky.

Eliza parked her car a quarter-mile down the private access road, concealing it behind a stand of wind-bent pines. The last stretch she would cover on foot, using the storm and darkness as cover. Rain pelted her as she moved through the underbrush, soaking through her jacket despite the waterproof material. The wind howled off the ocean, carrying salt spray that stung her eyes and face.

She paused at the edge of the manicured lawn, assessing the property. The house was dark except for a faint glow from what appeared to be the kitchen area. A black SUV was parked in the circular driveway—not Nathan's usual vehicle, but one she recognized from the police department's unmarked fleet. Chief Wallace's.

So Nathan wasn't working alone tonight. The conspiracy was rallying its forces.

Eliza circled the property, staying within the tree line, looking for the best approach. The beach house was designed for views, with floor-to-ceiling windows along the ocean side. Normally a security liability, but an advantage for her reconnaissance. If she could get close enough without being seen, she could observe what was happening inside.

A gust of wind nearly knocked her off balance as she made her way down a steep path toward the ocean side of the house. The beach below had disappeared, swallowed by the storm surge that pushed waves against the base of the cliff. The house itself, built on reinforced concrete pilings, stood like an island in the tempest.

From this angle, Eliza could see into what appeared to be the main living area. The space was dimly lit by a single lamp, but it was enough to reveal three figures: Nathan, pacing near a stone fireplace; Chief Wallace, his bulk unmistakable even in silhouette; and a third person, seated in a chair, head slumped forward. Carey Bennett, the missing journalist.

Eliza's pulse quickened. Bennett was alive—or at least, had been recently enough to be brought here. But the journalist's posture suggested she was either unconscious or restrained.

Moving closer, using a landscaped terrace as cover, Eliza could now see that Bennett's hands were bound to the chair arms with what looked like zip ties. The journalist's head lolled to one side, but Eliza could see her chest rising and falling. Alive, then.

Nathan and Wallace appeared to be arguing, their gestures animated though their voices were lost to the storm. Nathan pointed repeatedly at Bennett, then at his watch. Wallace shook his head, jabbing a finger toward the windows, presumably referencing the weather.

They were disagreeing about timing. About when to make Bennett disappear.

Eliza needed to get closer, needed to hear what they were saying. The terrace wrapped around to a set of glass doors that likely led to the kitchen. If she could reach those doors undetected...

A sudden movement caught her eye. A fourth person emerged from what must be a hallway leading to other rooms. Mayor Richard Whitaker, his silver hair and patrician features unmistakable even through rain-streaked glass.

The full triumvirate of the conspiracy, gathered in one place. And Eliza, alone, with evidence obtained through questionable means and no official backup.

She reached for her phone to call James, then hesitated. The hospital was at least thirty minutes away in good weather, longer in this storm. By the time help arrived, Bennett might be beyond saving. And calling for official backup would mean explaining how she knew where to find the journalist—revealing her illegal search of Nathan's office.

No, she would have to handle this herself. At least long enough to keep Bennett alive until legitimate help could arrive.

Eliza drew her service weapon and moved toward the kitchen doors, using shrubbery and patio furniture as cover. The wind worked in her favor now, howling so loudly that her approach was masked even when a branch snapped beneath her foot.

At the doors, she pressed herself against the wall of the house, peering carefully through the glass. The kitchen was empty, though she could see signs of recent use—a kettle on the stove, mugs on the counter. She tested the handle. Locked, as expected.

There was a keypad beside the door—a security system. Nathan would use the same code as his office safe, his pattern-oriented mind preferring consistency. Eliza entered 1-9-8-7.

Nothing happened.

She tried again: 5-7-0-4.

Still nothing.

A third attempt would likely trigger an alarm. She needed another approach.

The sound of raised voices drifted from the main room, becoming audible as the wind momentarily died down.

"—can't wait any longer," Nathan was saying. "The pattern must be maintained."

"The pattern is your obsession, not a necessity," Wallace replied. "No one's going out in this storm. The roads are flooded, the beach is underwater. We wait until conditions improve."

"And risk her regaining consciousness? Talking? She knows too much already."

"Then you should have handled this days ago, before she connected the dots." This from Whitaker, his tone imperious. "Your five-year schedule is arbitrary, Nathan. A psychological crutch."

"It's worked for thirty years," Nathan snapped. "No one suspected a pattern until Eliza, and that's only because of her memory. The timing is essential to the cover story—suicides and accidents during storm season, bodies never recovered. The perfect disappearances."

Eliza's blood ran cold at the casual way Nathan discussed making people vanish. The man who had counseled her through grief, who had been a father figure, who was about to become her stepfather—discussing murder as if it were a scheduling inconvenience.

"Speaking of Eliza," Wallace said, "where is she now?"

"With her mother, I assume. I've laid the groundwork with Patricia—suggested Eliza is having a psychological break, fixating on conspiracy theories about her father's death. When Eliza disappears, Patricia will believe she had a breakdown, maybe took her own life during the storm."

"And if she found something at your office?" Whitaker asked. "You said yourself she's been investigating the cold cases."

"Impossible. My records are secure."

"You underestimate her," Wallace said. "She's her father's daughter. Thomas was getting too close before his unfortunate accident. Eliza has already connected more dots than he ever did."

"Which is why she needs to be dealt with," Nathan replied. "Tonight. After we finish with Ms. Bennett."

They were planning to kill her. Not just make her disappear like the others, but actively planning her death. And her mother would be told she had suffered a breakdown, maybe committed suicide—the perfect cover story, just like the others.

Eliza's hand tightened on her weapon. She needed to act now, before they harmed Bennett further. But three against one, in an unfamiliar location, with a hostage in the middle—the tactical disadvantage was severe.

She needed a distraction.

The security system. If she could trigger it without being seen, the alarm might create enough confusion for her to gain entry and take control of the situation.

Eliza examined the keypad more closely. It was a standard model with a panic button at the bottom—designed to allow homeowners to trigger the alarm manually in an emergency. If she could activate it from outside...

She looked around for something to use. A heavy ceramic planter sat nearby, part of the terrace landscaping. It would be noisy, but that was the point.

Eliza lifted the planter with effort, positioned herself, and hurled it through the glass door. The crash was spectacular, shards flying in all directions as the alarm immediately began to wail—a piercing electronic shriek that cut through even the storm's fury.

She ducked to the side of the door, weapon ready, waiting for the response she knew would come.

Footsteps pounded toward the kitchen. "What the hell?" Wallace's voice.

"Security breach," Nathan called. "Check the perimeter. I'll stay with our guest."

Perfect. They were separating.

Eliza waited, counting silently. One. Two. Three.

Wallace appeared in the kitchen doorway, service weapon drawn, scanning the broken door and surrounding terrace. He stepped carefully through the shattered glass, moving onto the terrace.

"Police! Don't move!" Eliza emerged from her position, weapon trained on Wallace's broad back.

The police chief froze, then slowly turned. Recognition, then calculation, crossed his weathered face. "Detective Morgan. This is a surprise."

"Drop your weapon, Chief. Hands where I can see them."

Wallace made no move to comply. "You're making a serious mistake, Eliza. Whatever you think is happening here—"

"I know exactly what's happening. You, Nathan, and the mayor are holding Carey Bennett against her will. Planning to make her disappear, just like the others. Just like you did with my father."

"Your father's death was an accident."

"Save it. I have Nathan's journals. The evidence from his office. I know about the environmental cover-up, the contamination at the marina, the conspiracy to silence anyone who discovered the truth."

Something shifted in Wallace's expression—surprise, then resignation. "Then you understand why we can't let you leave."

"Drop the weapon, Chief. Last warning."

For a moment, Eliza thought he might comply. Then his eyes flicked to something behind her.

She started to turn, but too late. Pain exploded at the base of her skull, and darkness swallowed her consciousness.

Eliza awoke to the taste of blood and the sound of voices arguing. Her head throbbed where she'd been struck, and her vision swam as she tried to focus. She was seated, her hands secured behind her back with what felt like her own handcuffs. Her service weapon was gone.

"—completely unnecessary," Nathan was saying. "We had a system that worked. Clean. Clinical. No bodies, no evidence."

"Your system is compromised," Whitaker replied. "She knows everything. Found your trophies, your journals. We need to clean this up permanently."

"And how do you suggest we explain two bodies? A detective and a journalist, both investigating the marina project, both dead on the same night?"

"We don't explain anything. Storm victims, swept away. Tragic, but not suspicious."

Eliza kept her head down, feigning continued unconsciousness while she assessed her situation. She was in the main living area of the beach house, seated in a chair similar to the one holding Carey Bennett, who was now awake and watching the proceedings with terrified eyes.

Wallace stood by the fireplace, Eliza's service weapon in his hand. Nathan paced near the windows, while Whitaker sat in an armchair, looking for all the world like he was presiding over a town council meeting rather than a murder conspiracy.

"She'll have told someone," Nathan said. "Her partner, Harlow."

"Harlow is in the hospital," Wallace replied. "Brake line accident, remember? He's not a threat tonight."

"Her mother, then."

"Who believes her daughter is having a psychological break, thanks to your groundwork," Whitaker said dismissively. "No one will take her seriously if she starts talking about conspiracy theories."

Eliza's mind raced. They didn't know she had moved her mother to safety. Didn't know she had copied the evidence from Nathan's office. Small advantages, but she needed more.

She tested her restraints subtly. The handcuffs were secure, but her ankles were free. Her backup weapon—her father's revolver—was in an ankle holster, concealed by her pant leg. If she could reach it...

"She's awake," Wallace said suddenly, noticing her movement.

Eliza raised her head, meeting Nathan's gaze directly. "Hello, Nathan. Quite a storm tonight. Perfect for making people disappear."

Nathan's expression was a study in contrasts—the professional mask of calm concern overlaid with cold calculation. "Eliza. I wish it hadn't come to this. I genuinely cared for you and your mother."

"Spare me the sentimentality. You killed my father."

"Your father was becoming problematic. His environmental report threatened everything we'd built. The marina development was going to put Maplewood Bay on the map—bring in tourism, raise property values, create jobs. We couldn't let one flawed study derail decades of planning."

"Flawed? The contamination was real. Is real. You're building luxury condos on toxic land."

"The contamination was manageable," Whitaker interjected. "The remediation costs, however, would have bankrupted the project. We made a business decision."

"A business decision that killed six people. Seven, counting my father. And now you're planning to add two more to the list." Eliza glanced at Carey Bennett, who was watching the exchange with wide eyes. "Did Ms. Bennett find the same report my father did? The one Sarah Lindstrom discovered in the library archives?"

"Ms. Bennett was more thorough than that," Nathan said, almost proudly. "She found the connection between all the disappearances. Started asking questions about the five-year intervals. Even interviewed Martha Lindstrom about Sarah's journal."

"You should have been more careful with your pattern," Eliza said. "Five years exactly. Very consistent. Almost compulsive."

Nathan's eye twitched slightly at the psychological assessment. "Consistency creates plausibility. Random disappearances raise questions. A pattern, once recognized, suggests intention. But spaced properly, with the right cover stories, no one looks deeper."

"Except me."

"Except you," he agreed. "Your memory. Your father's determination. A dangerous combination."

"Enough reminiscing," Wallace interrupted. "We need to finish this and get out before the storm brings emergency services to the area."

"How are you going to explain shooting a detective with her own weapon?" Eliza asked, stalling for time. "Ballistics will match. Internal Affairs will investigate."

"You won't be shot," Nathan said calmly. "You and Ms. Bennett will be victims of the storm surge. Your bodies may never be recovered, like the others. But if they are, the medical examiner will find water in your lungs. A tragic drowning during a record storm."

The clinical detachment in his voice chilled Eliza more than any threat could have. This was a man who had orchestrated multiple deaths without remorse, who had counseled grieving families while knowing he had caused their pain.

"My mother will never believe I drowned accidentally. She knows I'm investigating you."

"Patricia believes you're having a breakdown," Nathan replied. "Fixating on conspiracy theories, making irrational connections. When you disappear during the storm, she'll assume you took your own life. Just like we arranged for the others."

"You've thought of everything," Eliza said, shifting slightly in her chair, trying to work her bound hands lower behind her back. "Except one thing."

"And what's that?" Whitaker asked, impatient.

"I'm not the only one with evidence against you. I made copies. Sent them to secure locations. If I don't check in by morning, they go to the State Police, the FBI, and the environmental protection agency."

It was a bluff, but a calculated one. She had copied Nathan's journals and photographed the evidence, but hadn't had time to secure or distribute the copies.

Uncertainty flickered across Nathan's face. "You're lying."

"Am I? You've known me since I was a teenager, Nathan. You know how thorough I am. How detail-oriented." Eliza leaned forward slightly. "Did you really think I wouldn't have a contingency plan?"

Nathan and Wallace exchanged glances. Whitaker stood, agitated.

"We need to know where those copies are," the mayor said. "Before we proceed."

"I'll tell you," Eliza replied. "But only after you release Ms. Bennett. She's not part of this."

"She's as much a threat as you are," Wallace growled.

"But not as valuable for leverage," Eliza countered. "You need me to cooperate if you want those copies. Ms. Bennett is just a liability now."

It was a desperate gambit, but Eliza could see the calculation happening behind Nathan's eyes. He was weighing options, probabilities, scenarios—just as he had taught her to do during therapy sessions after her father's death.

"She has a point," Nathan said finally. "Ms. Bennett is a complication we don't need. If Eliza has indeed distributed evidence, we need her cooperation."

"And you believe she'll cooperate after we release her only bargaining chip?" Whitaker scoffed. "She's playing for time."

"Of course I am," Eliza admitted. "But that doesn't make my offer less valid. Release Bennett, and I'll tell you where the copies are."

Nathan studied her for a long moment, then nodded to Wallace. "Cut Ms. Bennett loose. But don't release her yet. Not until we verify Eliza's information."

Wallace hesitated, then holstered Eliza's weapon and moved to Bennett, producing a pocketknife to cut the zip ties binding her wrists.

The journalist rubbed her chafed skin, eyes darting between her captors and Eliza.

"Now," Nathan turned back to Eliza. "Where are the copies?"

Eliza had managed to work her bound hands lower behind her back, almost to her ankles. Just a few more inches and she could reach her father's revolver.

"There's a USB drive in my apartment," she said, continuing to work her hands downward. "Hidden inside a hollowed-out copy of 'Crime and Punishment' on my bookshelf. The digital copies are there."

Nathan raised an eyebrow. "A bit on the nose, don't you think?"

"I have a fondness for the classics. And irony."

"And the physical copies? The photographs you took in my office?"

"Safe deposit box at Maplewood Community Bank. Key is in my desk drawer at the station."

Nathan nodded, seemingly satisfied. "Richard, take Ms. Bennett to the car. We'll need to verify Eliza's information before deciding her fate."

"And go where, exactly?" Whitaker gestured toward the windows, where the storm continued to rage. "The roads are flooded."

"We'll wait it out here," Nathan decided. "Keep them separated. Ms. Bennett in the guest room, Eliza here where we can watch her."

As Whitaker roughly pulled Bennett to her feet, Eliza made her move. In one fluid motion, she dropped from the chair to her knees, hands reaching behind her to grab the revolver from her ankle holster.

Wallace reacted instantly, reaching for Eliza's service weapon. But she was faster, bringing the revolver around and firing in one motion.

The shot went wide, shattering a window behind Wallace. The sudden inrush of wind and rain created momentary chaos. Bennett took advantage, driving her elbow into Whitaker's solar plexus and breaking free of his grasp.

"Run!" Eliza shouted to the journalist, firing again to provide cover.

This shot found its mark, catching Wallace in the shoulder. He staggered back, dropping Eliza's service weapon. Nathan dove for it, but Bennett was closer, scooping it up as she fled toward the kitchen and the broken door beyond.

Whitaker recovered quickly, producing a small handgun from inside his jacket. "Enough of this," he snarled, aiming at Eliza.

She rolled behind a sofa as his shot splintered the wooden floor where she had been kneeling. Her position was precarious—hands still cuffed behind her back, limited mobility, three armed opponents.

But Bennett had escaped. That was something.

"Eliza, be reasonable," Nathan called from behind the fireplace mantel where he had taken cover. "This can still end without further bloodshed."

"Like it did for my father? For Melissa Canning? For all the others you made disappear?" Eliza worked her way toward the edge of the sofa, trying to keep track of all three men. "It ends tonight, Nathan. One way or another."

"Your father was a good man who made a bad choice," Nathan replied, his voice taking on the soothing cadence he used with patients. "He discovered the contamination, yes. But he also agreed to suppress his findings when he understood what was at stake for the town."

This revelation hit Eliza like a physical blow. "You're lying."

"Am I? Look at the photograph in my office. Your father with us at the hunting cabin. He was part of the group, Eliza. Part of the development consortium. He only changed his mind later, threatened to expose everything when he realized the contamination was worse than initially reported."

Could it be true? Had her father been complicit before turning whistleblower? The doubt crept in, unwelcome but persistent.

"Even if that's true," she said, "it doesn't justify murder."

"We offered him money. A new start somewhere else. He refused." Nathan's voice hardened. "He chose his fate, Eliza. Just as you're choosing yours now."

A sudden crash from the kitchen interrupted the standoff. Bennett had returned, and she wasn't alone. Through the broken door came James Harlow, moving awkwardly with a makeshift crutch, his service weapon drawn.

"Police! Drop your weapons!" James's voice boomed through the house.

Wallace, bleeding from his shoulder wound, raised his hands slowly. Whitaker hesitated, then placed his gun on the floor.

Nathan, however, made a break for the hallway leading to the bedrooms. Eliza lunged after him, hampered by her bound hands but driven by determination. She caught him at the threshold, tackling him to the ground despite her restraints.

They struggled, Nathan's greater size and free hands giving him the advantage. He flipped her onto her back, hands closing around her throat.

"You're just like your father," he hissed, fingers tightening. "Too stubborn to know when to let go."

Eliza's vision began to darken at the edges as Nathan cut off her air supply. She bucked and twisted, but couldn't break his grip.

Then, suddenly, the pressure was gone. Nathan's weight lifted off her as James, balancing precariously on his good leg, dragged him backward.

"It's over, Wells," James said, pressing his weapon to Nathan's temple. "Thirty years of secrets. All exposed tonight."

Eliza gasped for air, rolling onto her side. Through the doorway, she could see Wallace and Whitaker being secured by Bennett, who had apparently found zip ties to return the favor her captors had shown her.

"How did you find us?" Eliza asked James as he handcuffed Nathan.

"Bennett called me from the kitchen before coming back in. Said a detective named Morgan was in trouble at Wells' beach house." James smiled grimly. "I was already on my way—checked myself out of the hospital when you didn't call back. Figured you'd found trouble, as usual."

"My mother—"

"Is safe. I sent a patrol car to the Pinecrest Motel to keep watch. Anonymous tip about a potential witness needing protection."

Relief washed over Eliza. Her mother was safe. Bennett was alive. The conspiracy exposed.

And Nathan—the man she had trusted, who had helped shape her into the detective she became—was revealed as the architect of decades of deception and death.

As James helped her to her feet, unlocking her handcuffs with his key, Eliza looked at Nathan. The professional mask had cracked completely, revealing the cold calculation beneath. He met her gaze without flinching.

"You won't be able to prove most of it," he said quietly. "The evidence is circumstantial. My journals could be dismissed as fiction, the ravings of a disturbed mind. Your illegal search of my office makes anything you found inadmissible."

"Maybe," Eliza acknowledged. "But Carey Bennett is alive to testify about her kidnapping. Chief Wallace and Mayor Whitaker will be looking to cut deals. And the environmental contamination can be verified now—no more cover-ups."

"The pattern ends tonight," James added, securing Nathan to a chair as sirens became audible in the distance. Emergency services, finally making their way through the storm.

"The pattern," Nathan repeated, a strange smile playing at his lips. "Five years. Always five years between disappearances. Did you ever wonder why, Eliza? Why that specific interval?"

Something in his tone made her pause. "Tell me."

"Five years is the statute of limitations for most environmental violations in this state. Each time someone discovered the truth, we silenced them, then waited for the legal vulnerability to expire before proceeding with the next phase of development." His smile widened. "Even our crimes were carefully planned around the law."

The calculated precision of it—the cold legal logic behind the timing of murders—sent a chill through Eliza that had nothing to do with the storm raging outside.

"You were my therapist," she said, the personal betrayal suddenly overwhelming the professional one. "You helped me through my grief after my father died. Grief you caused."

"And I did help you," Nathan replied, unrepentant. "You became stronger, more focused. A better detective than your father ever was. In a way, his death served a purpose beyond protecting our interests. It shaped you."

Eliza stepped closer, fighting the urge to strike him. "You don't get to claim credit for who I became. Not after what you did."

"But I do, Eliza. We're connected now, more deeply than you realize. Your father's death, your mother's trust, your own development—I've influenced it all. And now, even as you think you've won, you're still playing a role in my design."

"What are you talking about?"

Nathan leaned forward, lowering his voice conspiratorially. "Did you really think the contamination was limited to the marina? That the environmental damage could be contained to one convenient development site?" He laughed softly. "Your father's original report identified seven contaminated areas throughout Maplewood Bay. The marina was just Area 7—the most visible, the most valuable. The others remain hidden, ticking time bombs beneath schools, parks, residential neighborhoods."

Eliza felt the blood drain from her face. "You're lying again."

"Am I? Check your father's original data. The complete report, not the redacted version that's been circulating. Seven contaminated areas, Eliza. Seven secrets still buried."

Before she could respond, the front door burst open as State Police tactical officers swarmed into the beach house, responding to James's call for backup. The moment for private revelation was gone, replaced by the procedural machinery of justice.

As Nathan was led away, he turned back to Eliza one last time. "This isn't over," he called. "The pattern may end, but the consequences are just beginning. For all of us."

Eliza watched him go, the weight of his final revelation settling over her like the storm clouds that continued to churn above the beach house. Seven contaminated areas. Seven secrets still buried.

The case wasn't closed. It was just beginning.

And somewhere in Maplewood Bay, her father's complete environmental report waited to be found—the final piece of a puzzle thirty years in the making.

Dawn broke over Maplewood Bay, the storm finally exhausted after a night of fury. Eliza stood on the hospital roof, watching the sun illuminate a landscape transformed by water and wind. Trees down, roads flooded, boats tossed onto shore like discarded toys.

But the town still stood. Damaged, but not destroyed.

Like the truth she had uncovered—incomplete, but not entirely hidden any longer.

James joined her at the railing, his leg properly casted now, crutches tucked under his arms. "Quite a view," he observed. "You can see all the way to the marina from here."

The marina. Ground zero for the conspiracy that had claimed so many lives, including her father's. From this height, it looked peaceful, the water reflecting the morning light.

"Wallace is talking," James continued. "Cutting a deal with the district attorney. Whitaker too. They're falling over each other to be the first to confess in exchange for leniency."

"And Nathan?"

"Silent. His lawyer advised against any statements." James shifted his weight, wincing slightly. "But it doesn't matter. We have enough without his cooperation. Bennett's testimony, the kidnapping, the assault on you. That's enough to put him away for decades."

"But not for the disappearances. Not for my father."

"No," James admitted. "Not without more evidence. The journals you found might help, but as Nathan pointed out, they could be dismissed as fiction. And anything from his office is problematic given how you obtained it."

Eliza had already considered this. The legal case against Nathan for the historical crimes would be difficult to prove. But she had something else now—a new lead, a new purpose.

"He mentioned seven contaminated areas," she said. "My father's original report identified seven sites, not just the marina."

"And you believe him? After everything?"

"I believe he wanted to plant doubt. To ensure that even in defeat, he maintained some control over the narrative." Eliza turned to face James. "But that doesn't mean he was lying. Nathan's most effective manipulations always contained elements of truth."

"So what now? You go looking for this complete report?"

"Yes. And for the other contaminated sites. If they exist, people need to know. Need to be protected."

James studied her for a moment. "You know this could take years. Environmental investigations, legal battles, political resistance. The marina development has powerful backers beyond just Whitaker and his cronies."

"I have time," Eliza said simply. "And I have my father's determination."

"And his memory," James added with a small smile. "Both kinds—the one you inherited, and the one you're honoring."

Eliza nodded, turning back to the view. Somewhere in Maplewood Bay, seven secrets remained buried. Seven threats to public safety hidden by those who valued profit over people.

She would find them all. No matter how long it took.

The pattern of five-year disappearances had ended. But a new pattern was beginning—one of discovery, of truth, of justice delayed but not denied.

And this time, Eliza would be the one controlling the narrative.

Chapter 7: The Storm

Three weeks after the confrontation at Nathan's beach house, Maplewood Bay was still recovering from the physical and metaphorical storms that had swept through the coastal town. Fallen trees had been cleared, flooded streets had drained, and power had been restored to all but the most remote areas. But the emotional landscape remained forever altered.

Eliza Morgan stood at the edge of her father's grave, a simple granite marker in the hillside cemetery overlooking the bay. She hadn't visited in years, finding the ritual empty when compared to the vivid memories she carried within her. But today felt different. Today, she had answers.

"You were right," she said softly, placing a single white rose on the weathered stone. "About the contamination. About the cover-up. About all of it."

The morning air was crisp with early autumn, leaves beginning to turn on the maples that gave the town its name. In the distance, the marina glittered in the sunlight, deceptively peaceful. Construction on the expansion project had been halted pending environmental review—the first visible consequence of the conspiracy's exposure.

"They're going to test the soil again," Eliza continued, as if her father could hear. "The EPA is sending a team next week. No more cover-ups, no more falsified reports."

The investigation into Nathan Wells, James Wallace, and Richard Whitaker had dominated regional news for weeks. The story had everything—corruption, environmental crimes, kidnapping, attempted murder, and a three-decade conspiracy involving the town's most prominent citizens. Reporters descended on Maplewood Bay like locusts, digging into every aspect of the case.

But they didn't have what Eliza had—the personal connection, the perfect memory, and now, a new mission.

Seven contaminated areas. Seven secrets still buried.

"I'm going to find them all," she promised the silent grave. "Every site you identified. Make sure they're cleaned up properly this time."

"Talking to ghosts, Detective Morgan?"

Eliza turned to find Carey Bennett approaching along the gravel path, a leather messenger bag slung over her shoulder. The journalist looked remarkably recovered from her ordeal, though a fading bruise still colored her left cheekbone.

"Not ghosts. Just my father." Eliza gestured to the headstone. "Updating him on the case."

Bennett smiled. "I think he knows. Wherever he is, I think he's seen what you've done."

"What we've done," Eliza corrected. "Your article broke the story wide open."

Bennett's exposé in the Boston Globe had been comprehensive and damning, detailing the thirty-year conspiracy to cover up toxic contamination at the Maplewood Bay Marina. The piece had triggered investigations by state and federal authorities, class-action lawsuits from residents, and a political earthquake that had toppled half the town council.

"I had good sources," Bennett said, patting her messenger bag. "Speaking of which, I found something you might be interested in."

They walked together to a bench overlooking the bay, the marina visible in the distance. Bennett removed a manila folder from her bag and handed it to Eliza.

"County records from 1985," she explained. "Buried in the archives under miscellaneous environmental surveys. Someone tried to purge them, but missed this copy."

Eliza opened the folder to find a faded map of Maplewood Bay, with seven areas circled in red. Each was numbered and accompanied by handwritten notes in her father's distinctive script.

"The original survey," she breathed. "The complete report."

"All seven contaminated sites," Bennett confirmed. "The marina was just Area 7—the most visible because of the development plans. But your father identified six others, scattered throughout the town."

Eliza studied the map, memorizing each location. A former industrial site near the high school. A filled-in quarry where a playground now stood. An old military storage facility converted to apartments. A stream running behind the hospital. A vacant lot downtown. And a section of the beach on the north shore—near Nathan's house.

"Have you shown this to anyone else?" she asked.

Bennett shook her head. "Not yet. I wanted you to see it first. It's your father's work, after all."

"This changes everything," Eliza said, tracing the circles with her finger. "The scope of the contamination, the number of people potentially affected..."

"The liability," Bennett added. "The development corporation could be facing billions in damages and cleanup costs. Not to mention the criminal charges for knowingly building on toxic land."

Eliza thought of Nathan, currently held without bail while awaiting trial for kidnapping and attempted murder. He had maintained his silence, refusing to cooperate with investigators or implicate others beyond those already arrested. But this map—this evidence from thirty years ago—might finally break his composure.

"I need to take this to the district attorney," Eliza said, carefully returning the map to its folder. "And to the EPA team when they arrive."

"I thought you might say that." Bennett smiled. "That's why I brought you the original. I have copies for my follow-up article."

"You're still investigating?"

"Of course. This story is far from over." Bennett's expression turned serious. "The conspiracy may have been exposed, but the consequences are just beginning. People have been living on contaminated land for decades, Eliza. The health implications alone..."

"I know." Eliza had been thinking about little else since Nathan's revelation about the seven sites. How many illnesses might be traced back to the toxins? How many lives affected beyond those directly silenced by the conspiracy?

"There's something else," Bennett said, hesitating. "Something I haven't put in my articles yet. About Nathan Wells."

Eliza tensed. "What about him?"

"I've been researching his background. Before he came to Maplewood Bay, he worked for a chemical company—Northstar Industries. They specialized in industrial solvents, the same compounds found in the marina soil samples."

The implication was clear. "You think he knew about the contamination before my father's report? That he was involved from the beginning?"

"I think it's a hell of a coincidence that a chemist-turned-psychologist ended up as the point person for silencing whistleblowers about chemical contamination." Bennett pulled another document from her bag—a staff photo from Northstar Industries, dated 1982. "Look who else worked there."

Eliza scanned the faces in the faded photograph, stopping at a familiar figure in the back row. James Wallace, three decades younger but unmistakable.

"Wallace and Nathan knew each other before Maplewood Bay," she murmured. "They came here together."

"And within five years, they were both in positions of influence—Nathan as the town's leading psychologist, Wallace rising quickly through the police department ranks." Bennett took back the photo. "I don't think the contamination was an accident, Eliza. I think it was deliberate."

The theory was staggering in its implications. Not negligence or a cover-up after the fact, but intentional environmental sabotage, followed by a decades-long conspiracy to hide the evidence and silence witnesses.

"Why?" Eliza asked. "What could possibly be worth that kind of risk?"

"Money, of course. The development corporation purchased the land for pennies on the dollar after it was contaminated. Property values in surrounding areas plummeted temporarily, allowing them to acquire huge swaths of the coastline. Once the contamination was covered up and development began, those same properties increased in value by thousands of percent."

"Creating millions in profit," Eliza finished. "Billions, eventually."

"Exactly. The perfect crime—poison the land, buy it cheap, hide the evidence, develop it, and get rich." Bennett's eyes gleamed with the intensity of a journalist onto a career-making story. "And it would have worked if your father hadn't discovered the truth."

Eliza thought of her father—his integrity, his determination to do what was right despite the pressure to look the other way. He had paid the ultimate price for that integrity.

"I need to see Nathan," she said suddenly.

Bennett looked surprised. "He's not talking to anyone. His lawyer has shut down all interview requests."

"He'll talk to me." Eliza stood, tucking the folder securely under her arm. "There's unfinished business between us."

The Maplewood Bay Detention Center was a modern facility on the outskirts of town, its bland architecture belying the human drama contained within its walls. Eliza had visited countless times in her professional capacity, but never to see someone she had once considered family.

Nathan Wells sat across from her in the visitation room, separated by a plexiglass partition. Prison hadn't diminished his dignified bearing—he sat straight-backed in the orange jumpsuit, hands folded neatly on the table before him. Only the shadows under his eyes suggested any distress at his circumstances.

"Eliza," he greeted her, voice calm. "I wondered when you'd come."

"I've been busy," she replied. "Cleaning up your mess."

A slight smile touched his lips. "Our mess, perhaps. Your father was involved too, remember."

"As a whistleblower. Not as a conspirator."

"Is that what you need to believe?" Nathan's gaze was penetrating, the psychologist still analyzing even from behind bars. "That Thomas was purely a victim, never complicit?"

"I know what you're doing," Eliza said. "Trying to plant doubt. To maintain some control over the narrative. It won't work anymore."

She placed the folder against the plexiglass, open to show the map with its seven circled areas. "I found my father's complete report. All seven contaminated sites, just as you said."

Nathan's expression didn't change, but Eliza caught the slight dilation of his pupils—surprise, quickly masked.

"Congratulations," he said evenly. "Though I'm not sure what you expect me to say."

"I want the truth. About Northstar Industries. About you and Wallace deliberately contaminating the land before coming to Maplewood Bay."

This time, Nathan couldn't hide his reaction—a momentary widening of the eyes, a tightening of his folded hands.

"Ah," he said after a pause. "Ms. Bennett has been thorough in her research."

"Was it true? Did you poison the land intentionally?"

Nathan studied her for a long moment, as if deciding how much to reveal. "Would it matter if I did? The charges I'm facing already ensure I'll spend the rest of my life in prison. What difference would one more crime make?"

"It would matter to the victims. To the families of those who disappeared. To my mother."

At the mention of Patricia, something flickered in Nathan's eyes—the first genuine emotion Eliza had seen from him.

"How is she?" he asked quietly.

"Devastated. Betrayed. Trying to reconcile the man she loved with the monster you turned out to be."

Nathan flinched slightly at the word "monster." "I never wanted to hurt Patricia. Or you, for that matter. You were... unexpected complications in an otherwise straightforward operation."

"An operation that involved multiple murders."

"Necessary removals of threats to a greater purpose." Nathan leaned forward. "You still don't understand the full scope, Eliza. This was never just about money."

"Then explain it to me."

Nathan glanced at the security camera in the corner of the room, then back at Eliza. "Not here. Not now. But I'll make you a deal—you bring me something, and I'll tell you everything. The complete truth about Northstar, about your father, about why Maplewood Bay was chosen."

Eliza's instincts warned caution. "What do you want?"

"A book. From my office library. 'The Psychology of Environmental Perception' by Harland. Inside is a key to a safe deposit box at First National. The contents will explain everything."

"Why would I help you access anything?"

"Because the box doesn't contain money or escape plans, Eliza. It contains evidence. Documentation of the entire operation, from its inception to the present day. Names of everyone involved—not just Wallace and Whitaker, but corporate executives, federal officials, others you haven't even considered yet."

Eliza studied him, trying to detect deception. "Why would you keep evidence that could be used against you?"

"Insurance," Nathan said simply. "Against partners who might consider me expendable. And now, leverage. Bring me the key, and I'll sign a full confession. Every detail, every name, every crime."

It could be a trap. Or it could be the final piece of the puzzle—the evidence needed to ensure that everyone involved in the conspiracy faced justice.

"I'll think about it," Eliza said, gathering the folder.

"Don't think too long," Nathan replied. "There are people who would prefer that evidence never see the light of day. People with the resources and motivation to ensure it disappears—along with anyone looking for it."

"Is that a threat?"

"A warning. From someone who, despite everything, doesn't want to see you become the seventh disappearance."

Eliza stood to leave, but Nathan's voice stopped her.

"One more thing, Eliza. Your father's report identifies seven contaminated areas, but there's an eighth that he never documented. The most dangerous one of all."

"Where?"

Nathan smiled enigmatically. "Bring me the key, and I'll tell you. Consider it a gesture of good faith."

As Eliza left the detention center, the weight of Nathan's words pressed upon her. An eighth contamination site. More evidence hidden in a safe deposit box. The conspiracy extending beyond Maplewood Bay to corporate and federal levels.

The case that had seemed to be concluding was instead expanding, revealing new depths of corruption and danger.

And at the center of it all, still manipulating events even from behind bars, was Nathan Wells— the man who had helped shape her into the detective she had become, now offering one final lesson in the complexity of truth and deception.

"He's playing you," James Harlow said flatly, leaning on his crutches in Eliza's living room. "Classic manipulation—offering partial information to get what he wants, dangling the promise of 'the complete truth' like bait."

"I know," Eliza agreed, pacing restlessly. "But what if he's telling the truth about the evidence? About an eighth contamination site?"

"Then we find it ourselves. Without giving Nathan what he wants."

Eliza had invited James and Carey Bennett to her apartment to discuss Nathan's proposition. The three of them formed an unlikely alliance—the detective, the journalist, and the veteran cop—united by their connection to the conspiracy and its exposure.

"The safe deposit box is worth checking out," Bennett argued. "If it contains what he claims, it could break the case wide open. Implicate people we don't even know are involved."

"And if it's a trap?" James countered. "If there's nothing there, or worse, something that could compromise our existing case against him?"

"That's why we proceed carefully," Eliza said. "I'll get the book and the key, but we don't give Nathan anything until we've verified the contents of the box."

"You're assuming the bank will let you access it," James pointed out. "Safe deposit boxes require both the customer's key and the bank's key."

"I have contacts at First National," Bennett said. "If the box is evidence in an ongoing criminal investigation..."

"Which it technically isn't, since we don't know what's in it," James finished. "We'd need a warrant, which requires probable cause, which we don't have without knowing what's in the box. It's circular."

Eliza stopped pacing, a new thought occurring to her. "Unless the box isn't in Nathan's name. What if it's in my father's name? Or my mother's?"

The possibility hung in the air. Nathan had been engaged to Patricia, had been close to the Morgan family for years. He would have had access to their personal information, perhaps even their identification documents.

"That would be a whole new level of manipulation," Bennett said slowly. "Using your family's identity to hide evidence that could implicate him in your father's death."

"It would be consistent with his psychological profile," James admitted. "Nathan's entire modus operandi involves layers of deception and personal connection."

Eliza made her decision. "I'll get the book and the key. Bennett, check with your bank contacts about safe deposit boxes under the names Nathan Wells, Thomas Morgan, or Patricia Morgan. James, keep digging into Northstar Industries and its connection to Maplewood Bay."

"And the eighth contamination site?" Bennett asked.

"One mystery at a time," Eliza replied. "First, we see what's in that safe deposit box. Then we decide whether to trust anything else Nathan tells us."

As her colleagues left, Eliza turned to the map spread across her dining table—her father's original survey with its seven circled areas. Each represented a health risk to the people of Maplewood Bay, a ticking time bomb of toxic chemicals that had been ignored for three decades.

And somewhere, unmarked, was an eighth site—potentially more dangerous than all the others.

The storm that had raged the night of Nathan's arrest had passed, but Eliza could feel another gathering on the horizon. The conspiracy had deeper roots than anyone had imagined, extending beyond Maplewood Bay to corporate boardrooms and perhaps even government offices.

She traced the red circles on the map, her perfect memory cataloging each location and its proximity to schools, homes, water sources. How many people had been affected over the years? How many illnesses could be traced back to these hidden poisons?

The scope of the crime was staggering—not just the silencing of whistleblowers, but the deliberate endangerment of an entire community for profit.

And Nathan, the architect of so much suffering, was still controlling the flow of information, still manipulating events from his prison cell.

Eliza folded the map carefully, her resolve hardening. She would play his game, but on her terms. She would find the evidence, expose every person involved, and ensure that justice was served—not just for her father, but for all the victims of the Maplewood Bay conspiracy.

The storm was coming. And this time, she would be ready.

Nathan's office remained as he had left it the night of his arrest, sealed with police tape as a crime scene. Eliza had official access now, no need for lock picks or copied keys. The space felt different in daylight, less threatening but somehow more melancholy—the abandoned domain of a fallen authority figure.

She found the book easily on his professional bookshelf: "The Psychology of Environmental Perception" by Harland, a scholarly text that would interest few outside the field. Inside, as promised, was a small key taped to the back cover, unmarked except for the number 723.

Eliza photographed the key in place before removing it, documenting its discovery for the official record. Whatever happened next would be by the book—no more unauthorized searches or questionable methods. Too much was at stake.

Her phone buzzed with a text from Bennett: "Box confirmed at First National. Under T. Morgan's name. Accessed regularly until 2017."

So Nathan had used her father's identity, continuing to access the box decades after Thomas Morgan's death. The violation felt personal, another layer of betrayal in a case already full of them.

Eliza pocketed the key and left the office, sealing it again with fresh evidence tape. As she walked to her car, she noticed a black sedan parked across the street, its windows tinted beyond legal limits. The vehicle hadn't been there when she arrived.

She memorized the license plate automatically, her training kicking in. The plate was from out of state—Virginia. Not a local, then. And not trying very hard to remain inconspicuous.

A warning? Or simple surveillance?

Either way, it confirmed Nathan's claim that others were interested in the evidence he had hidden. People with resources and motivation to ensure it remained buried.

Eliza drove directly to the police station, taking a circuitous route to determine if she was being followed. The black sedan didn't appear again, but she couldn't shake the feeling of being watched.

At the station, she filed the key into evidence, documenting its discovery and requesting a formal warrant to access the safe deposit box registered to Thomas Morgan at First National Bank. The process would take time—hours, maybe days—but it would be legal, transparent, and admissible in court.

While waiting for the warrant, Eliza turned her attention to Northstar Industries. The company had ceased operations in 1990, its assets acquired by a larger chemical conglomerate. Corporate records from that era were sparse, but Bennett had obtained employment files confirming that both Nathan Wells and James Wallace had worked there from 1980 to 1985—Nathan as a research chemist, Wallace as head of security.

They had arrived in Maplewood Bay within months of each other in 1985—the same year Thomas Morgan had conducted his environmental survey identifying seven contaminated areas.

The timing couldn't be coincidental. But what was the connection? Why target Maplewood Bay specifically?

Eliza pulled up old maps of the town and surrounding county, looking for anything that might explain the choice. Maplewood Bay was picturesque but unremarkable—a small coastal community with modest tourism, some fishing industry, and little else of economic significance in the early 1980s.

Until she noticed something on a geological survey map from 1979: a proposed route for an interstate highway that would have connected Maplewood Bay directly to Boston, cutting travel time in half. The route had been abandoned in

1983 due to environmental concerns and local opposition.

But if that highway had been built, property values in Maplewood Bay would have skyrocketed. Waterfront land would have become prime real estate for development.

Was that the plan? Contaminate the land, tank property values, buy cheap, then push for the highway project to be revived once the toxins were safely covered up?

It made a certain cold economic sense. But the highway had never been built. The contaminated land had remained relatively worthless until the marina development began in the late 1990s.

Something was missing from the equation. Some factor that would explain why Nathan, Wallace, and their unnamed partners would take such an enormous risk for a payoff that never materialized as planned.

Eliza's phone rang—James, calling from home where he was recuperating from his injuries.

"I found something," he said without preamble. "Northstar wasn't just manufacturing industrial solvents. They had a government contract—Department of Defense. Classified research into chemical compounds for military applications."

"Weapons research?" Eliza asked, the implications immediately clear.

"Not officially. But the compounds they were developing had dual-use potential. And guess who was the lead scientist on the project?"

"Nathan."

"Bingo. His specialty was in chemicals that could be deployed in an urban environment without detection—colorless, odorless, with delayed health effects."

The perfect profile for the contaminants found at the marina site—and presumably at the other six locations around Maplewood Bay.

"They weren't just dumping industrial waste," Eliza realized. "They were testing the compounds. Using Maplewood Bay as a laboratory."

"That's my theory," James confirmed. "The property value angle was secondary—a way to profit from the experiment, but not the primary motivation."

"But why? Why risk exposure, criminal charges, everything—just to test these chemicals?"

"That's the million-dollar question. And I'm betting the answer is in that safe deposit box."

As if on cue, Eliza's desk phone rang. The warrant had been approved. She could access the box at First National as soon as a judge signed the final order—tomorrow morning at the latest.

"We're about to find out," she told James. "The warrant came through."

"Be careful, Eliza. If Nathan was involved in classified DoD research, this could go beyond local corruption. There could be national security implications."

"All the more reason to expose it," she replied. "Whatever's in that box, the truth needs to come out. For everyone affected by what they did to this town."

After hanging up, Eliza sat back, processing the new information. Maplewood Bay as a testing ground for military-grade chemicals. Seven—no, eight—contaminated sites strategically placed throughout the town. Decades of health impacts on an unwitting population.

The conspiracy had just expanded from environmental crime and murder to something approaching a war crime—the deliberate exposure of civilians to experimental chemical agents.

And tomorrow, she would have the evidence to prove it.

Unless someone stopped her first.

The black sedan was back, parked half a block from Eliza's apartment building when she returned home that evening. Still Virginia plates, still tinted windows, still making no effort to conceal its presence.

A message, then. Not "we're watching you" but "we want you to know we're watching you."

Eliza walked past without acknowledging the vehicle, but her senses were on high alert. Inside her building, she checked the stairwell and hallway carefully before approaching her apartment door.

No signs of forced entry, but that meant little with professionals. She entered cautiously, hand near her service weapon, clearing each room methodically.

The apartment was undisturbed, exactly as she had left it. But on her dining table, centered precisely on her father's map, was a small object that hadn't been there before.

A bird figurine. Metal, like the one Nathan had given her the night of the confrontation.

Someone had been inside her apartment—someone with access to the same tokens left at the scenes of the disappearances. Someone sending a very clear message about what happened to people who threatened the conspiracy.

Eliza photographed the bird in place, then carefully bagged it as evidence. She would have the apartment dusted for prints, though she expected none would be found. This was too professional, too deliberate.

She called James, updating him on the development.

"You need to stay somewhere else tonight," he insisted. "If they've been in your apartment once, they can come back."

"That's exactly what they want—to scare me off, delay access to the safe deposit box." Eliza was already checking her windows and doors, ensuring everything was secure. "I'm staying. But I won't be sleeping."

"At least call for a patrol car to watch the building."

"And alert whoever's in the sedan that I'm rattled? No. Better they think their intimidation tactic failed."

After hanging up, Eliza settled in for a long night. She positioned herself in the living room with clear sightlines to both the front door and fire escape window, her service weapon within easy reach.

As midnight approached, the black sedan remained in position outside. Whoever was watching was prepared for a lengthy surveillance.

Eliza's phone buzzed with a text from an unknown number: "Walk away. Last warning."

She didn't respond, didn't give them the satisfaction of knowing their message had been received. Instead, she continued her vigil, reviewing case notes and planning the next day's approach to the safe deposit box.

Around 2 AM, movement on the street caught her attention. The black sedan's door opened, and a figure emerged—tall, military bearing, nondescript dark clothing. The figure looked up directly at Eliza's window, as if knowing exactly where she was positioned, then walked purposefully toward her building.

Eliza tensed, gripping her weapon. This was it—the intimidation escalating to direct confrontation.

She heard the building's front door open, then footsteps on the stairs. Measured, unhurried steps of someone confident in their purpose.

The footsteps stopped outside her door. No knock, no attempt at subterfuge. Just silence, pregnant with threat.

Eliza aimed her weapon at the door, ready for whatever came next.

A white envelope slid under the door, then the footsteps retreated, descending the stairs with the same measured pace.

She waited until she heard the building door close, then approached the envelope cautiously. It could contain anything—a threat, a bribe, a toxic substance.

Using a pen, she flipped the envelope over. No markings, no address, no name. Just a plain white business envelope, sealed.

Eliza used a letter opener to slit the top, then carefully shook out the contents onto her coffee table.

Inside was a single photograph—old, slightly faded, but clear enough. It showed a group of men in lab coats standing before a sign reading "Northstar Industries - Special Projects Division."

In the center of the group was Nathan, younger but recognizable. Beside him stood James Wallace.

And on Nathan's other side, smiling at the camera, was Thomas Morgan. Her father.

The implication was unmistakable. Thomas hadn't just discovered the contamination as an independent environmental consultant. He had been part of Northstar—part of the team that had created the toxic compounds in the first place.

Eliza stared at the photo, her perfect memory cataloging every detail while her mind struggled to process the revelation. Her father—the man whose integrity she had never questioned, whose death she had attributed to his whistleblowing—had been involved from the beginning.

Was this genuine evidence, or another of Nathan's manipulations? A truth bomb designed to destabilize her at a critical moment?

She turned the photo over. On the back, handwritten in faded ink, was a note: "Northstar team celebrates Project Maplewood approval, 1984."

Project Maplewood. The town hadn't been randomly selected—it had been the designated target of whatever experiment Northstar had been conducting.

And her father had been part of it.

Eliza sank onto the couch, the photo still in her hand. Everything she thought she knew about the case, about her father, about her own motivation for pursuing justice—all of it was now in question.

Outside, the black sedan started its engine and pulled away from the curb. The message had been delivered. The psychological warfare had achieved its objective.

As dawn broke over Maplewood Bay, Eliza faced the most difficult decision of her career: proceed to the bank and open the safe deposit box, potentially exposing her father's complicity in the very crimes she had been investigating; or walk away, protecting his memory but allowing the full truth to remain buried.

The storm that had been gathering on the horizon had arrived. And it threatened to wash away not just the conspiracy, but the foundations of Eliza's identity as her father's daughter.

Chapter 8: The Truth

First light crept over Maplewood Bay, illuminating a town transformed. Not just by the storm that had ravaged its coastline the previous night, but by revelations that had shaken its foundations. Eliza Morgan stood at her apartment window, the photograph of her father with the Northstar team clutched in her hand, watching as emergency vehicles navigated flooded streets and crews worked to clear fallen trees.

The black sedan was gone from its surveillance position, its message delivered. Her father—the man whose integrity had shaped her life and career—had been part of Northstar Industries. Part of the team that had developed the toxic compounds later found in Maplewood Bay. The implications were staggering.

But was it true? Or another manipulation, designed to derail her investigation at a critical moment?

Eliza studied the photograph again, her perfect memory cataloging every detail. The date: July 1984. The location: Northstar's research facility in Virginia. The faces: Nathan Wells, James Wallace, and Thomas Morgan, along with five other men she didn't recognize. All smiling, celebrating "Project Maplewood."

If genuine, this photo predated her father's environmental survey by nearly a year. It suggested not just knowledge of the contamination, but potential involvement in its creation.

She set the photograph aside and picked up her phone. The warrant for Thomas Morgan's safe deposit box at First National had been approved late yesterday. In a few hours, she could access whatever Nathan had hidden there—evidence that might confirm or refute the photograph's implications.

But first, she needed perspective from someone who had known her father professionally.

Dr. Eleanor Chen answered on the third ring, her voice sleep-rough. "Eliza? It's not even seven AM."

"I'm sorry to call so early," Eliza said. "But I need to ask you about my father."

A pause. "I haven't thought about Thomas in years. What's this about?"

Dr. Chen had been the county's medical examiner when Thomas Morgan died. She had performed the autopsy, signed the death certificate listing cause as accidental drowning with alcohol as a contributing factor. She had also been one of the few people to question that finding, though never officially.

"Did my father ever mention Northstar Industries to you? Or a project called Maplewood?"

Another pause, longer this time. "Where did you hear those names?"

"So you do know them."

"Eliza, what's going on? This isn't a casual inquiry at dawn after a major storm."

Eliza hesitated, then decided on honesty. "I'm investigating a series of disappearances connected to environmental contamination at the marina. The trail leads back to Northstar Industries and a classified research project. I have evidence suggesting my father was involved."

Silence stretched between them. Finally, Dr. Chen sighed. "Not over the phone. Meet me at Harborview Café in an hour. And Eliza? Be careful who you trust with this."

The call ended, leaving Eliza with more questions than answers. Dr. Chen's reaction confirmed the names meant something—but what?

She showered and dressed quickly, choosing practical clothing suitable for a day that would likely involve both a bank visit and further investigation in weather-damaged areas. Her service weapon went into its holster, her father's revolver into her ankle holster. The photograph and her notes went into a waterproof messenger bag.

As she prepared to leave, her phone rang—James Harlow.

"Morning," she answered. "How's the leg?"

"Hurts like hell," James replied cheerfully. "But that's not why I'm calling. I've been digging into Northstar Industries. Found something interesting in declassified Defense Department records."

"I'm listening."

"Project Maplewood wasn't just about chemical development. It was a field test—a controlled experiment to study long-term exposure effects in a civilian population."

Eliza's blood ran cold. "They deliberately contaminated the town? As an experiment?"

"That's what the fragments I've found suggest. Most records are still classified, but there are references to 'Site M' as a 'longitudinal exposure study' with 'minimal demographic disruption.'"

"Meaning they poisoned people slowly enough that no one would notice the pattern."

"Exactly. And guess who was the project's environmental assessment officer? The person responsible for monitoring containment and exposure levels?"

Eliza closed her eyes. "My father."

"Thomas Morgan. His name is all over the redacted documents. He was part of it, Eliza."

The confirmation hit hard, despite her preparation for it. "I'm meeting Dr. Chen in an hour. She knew something when I mentioned Northstar."

"Eleanor Chen? The former ME? Be careful. We don't know who was involved."

"I will. I'm also accessing the safe deposit box today. Nathan claims it contains evidence about the entire operation."

"Want backup? I can hobble along dramatically. Might provide a good distraction."

Despite everything, Eliza smiled. "Thanks, but no. Your job is to keep digging into Northstar. Find out who else was involved, how high this goes."

"Already on it. And Eliza? Whatever your father did... people change. The man who raised you, who taught you about justice—that was real too."

After hanging up, Eliza stood motionless in her apartment, absorbing the implications. Her father had helped design an experiment that exposed an entire town to toxic chemicals. Had monitored the effects. Had been part of a conspiracy that later killed to protect its secrets.

And then he had tried to stop it. Had written the environmental report that threatened to expose everything. Had died for that choice.

Could both versions of Thomas Morgan be true? The scientist who participated in an unethical experiment and the father who had taught her about integrity and justice?

The photograph stared back at her from the table, its silent testimony damning. But photographs could lie. Context could be manipulated. The only certainty was that the safe deposit box might contain answers—if she could trust anything that came from Nathan Wells.

Eliza gathered her things and left the apartment, locking the door behind her. Whatever the truth about her father, she would face it. And then she would ensure that justice was served—for all the victims of Project Maplewood.

Harborview Café sat on a bluff overlooking the marina, its large windows offering panoramic views of the damage below. Boats had been tossed onto the shore like discarded toys. Debris littered the water. Emergency crews worked to secure loose vessels and assess structural damage to the docks.

Dr. Eleanor Chen sat at a corner table, her back to the wall, a cup of coffee cooling before her. At sixty-five, she remained striking—silver hair cut in a precise bob, posture military-straight, eyes sharp behind rimless glasses. She had retired five years ago, moving to Florida, but had returned for her granddaughter's high school graduation.

Fortuitous timing, or something else?

"Dr. Chen," Eliza greeted her, sliding into the opposite chair. "Thank you for meeting me."

"Eleanor, please. We're not in the morgue anymore." The older woman studied Eliza with clinical precision. "You look like him. Same intensity. Same inability to let things go."

"You knew my father well?"

"Well enough. We worked together occasionally—his environmental surveys, my public health concerns. Professional relationship mostly, but I respected him." She sipped her coffee. "Now tell me why you're asking about Northstar after all these years."

Eliza ordered coffee from a passing server, then leaned forward. "I'm investigating a series of disappearances spanning thirty years. All victims had discovered information about toxic contamination at the marina. All were silenced before they could expose it."

"Including Thomas."

"Yes. His brake lines were cut. The toxicology report was falsified to show alcohol in his system."

Eleanor nodded, unsurprised. "I suspected as much. The blood alcohol levels didn't match his liver enzymes. But my concerns were... discouraged."

"By Chief Wallace."

"Among others." Eleanor's gaze drifted to the marina below. "Your father was a complicated man, Eliza. Brilliant, principled in many ways, but also ambitious. Northstar offered him an opportunity few scientists could resist—unlimited funding, cutting-edge research, government backing."

"For a project that deliberately exposed civilians to toxic chemicals."

Eleanor's eyes snapped back to Eliza's face. "So you know about Project Maplewood."

"I know it existed. I know my father was involved. I know people have been killed to keep it secret." Eliza removed the photograph from her bag, sliding it across the table. "What I don't know is why. Why Maplewood Bay? Why these specific chemicals? What was the purpose?"

Eleanor studied the photograph, her expression unreadable. "This is genuine. I remember when it was taken—the celebration when the project received final approval." She looked up. "You're right about the experiment. Northstar developed chemical compounds for military applications—weapons that could incapacitate rather than kill, designed for urban warfare scenarios. But they needed data on long-term exposure effects."

"Human testing."

"Controlled environmental exposure. Seven sites around town, each with different concentration levels and delivery methods. The marina was Site 7—the control site with the highest concentration."

"And my father monitored the effects."

"Initially, yes. He designed the monitoring protocols, established baseline measurements. But about six months in, he began to notice concerning patterns. Health issues that weren't in the projected models. He wanted to modify the experiment, reduce exposure levels. When that was rejected, he advocated for termination."

"So he tried to stop it."

"He tried to contain it. There's a difference." Eleanor handed back the photograph. "Thomas believed he could mitigate the damage without exposing the project. He was naive."

"What changed? Why did he decide to write the environmental report that threatened to expose everything?"

Eleanor's expression softened slightly. "You did."

"Me?"

"You were diagnosed with asthma. Mild, but unexpected given your family history. Thomas connected it to the airborne compounds at Site 3—near your elementary school. That's when it became personal for him. When he realized the true cost of what he'd helped create."

Eliza sat back, processing this revelation. Her childhood asthma—long outgrown—had been caused by her father's own project. And had ultimately led to his death when he tried to expose the truth.

"The environmental report," she said slowly. "The complete version with all seven sites. He was going to go public with it?"

"Yes. He had compiled irrefutable evidence of the contamination and its health effects. Enough to shut down the project and trigger a federal investigation." Eleanor's voice lowered. "The night before he died, he called me. Said he had secured copies of everything—the original project documents, his monitoring data, health impact assessments. Said he had hidden it somewhere even Northstar couldn't find it."

"A safe deposit box at First National Bank."

Eleanor looked surprised. "He told you?"

"No. Nathan Wells told me. He's been using my father's identity to access it for years."

"Nathan." Eleanor's mouth tightened. "The perfect company man. Brilliant chemist, zero moral compass. He and your father were colleagues at Northstar before the project. Nathan recruited Thomas."

"And then arranged his death when he became a threat."

"I always suspected, but could never prove it." Eleanor checked her watch. "The bank opens in thirty minutes. Whatever Thomas hid there could finally expose the truth about Project Maplewood."

"Or it could be another manipulation. Nathan wants me to access that box for a reason."

"Of course he does. But that doesn't mean the contents aren't valuable." Eleanor stood, gathering her coat. "I'm coming with you."

"That's not necessary—"

"It wasn't a request, Detective Morgan. I've waited thirty years to learn what really happened to Thomas. I'm not missing it now."

First National Bank of Maplewood Bay occupied a stately brick building downtown, its colonial architecture projecting stability and trustworthiness. The lobby was quiet when Eliza and Eleanor entered, just a few customers conducting early morning business.

The bank manager, alerted to their arrival, met them personally—a courtesy extended to law enforcement executing a warrant, but also perhaps a recognition of the Morgan name. Thomas had been well-respected in Maplewood Bay before his death.

"Detective Morgan, Dr. Chen." The manager, a woman in her fifties named Helen Graves, greeted them with professional warmth. "I understand you're here about a safe deposit box registered to Thomas Morgan."

"Yes. I have a warrant authorizing access." Eliza presented the document, which Helen examined carefully.

"Everything appears in order. If you'll follow me to the vault area."

They were led through a secure door into a room lined with metal boxes of various sizes. Helen consulted her records. "Box 723. It's one of our larger models." She inserted her master key, then looked expectantly at Eliza. "I'll need the customer key as well."

Eliza produced the key from Nathan's book, noting how perfectly it matched the lock. This was indeed the correct box.

With both keys turned, the box slid out smoothly. Helen placed it on a private table in an adjacent room. "I'll give you privacy. Please ring the bell when you're finished."

When they were alone, Eliza stared at the metal container. Whatever it contained had been important enough for her father to hide, for Nathan to monitor for decades, and for unknown parties to threaten her over.

"Open it," Eleanor urged softly.

Eliza lifted the lid.

Inside was a single USB drive and a thick manila envelope. The envelope was labeled in her father's handwriting: "Project Maplewood—Complete Documentation."

With gloved hands, Eliza carefully opened the envelope. It contained hundreds of pages of documents—technical specifications, chemical formulas, maps of Maplewood Bay with the seven contamination sites clearly marked, health monitoring data spanning years, and internal Northstar memos discussing the project's progress.

Most damning were the authorization forms, bearing signatures from Northstar executives, Department of Defense officials, and local authorities who had permitted the experiment—including a younger James Wallace, then head of security for Northstar, and Richard Whitaker, already a rising political figure in town government.

"This is everything," Eleanor breathed, scanning the documents. "Enough to prove the deliberate contamination, the cover-up, the health impacts. Thomas really did compile it all."

Eliza's attention was drawn to a separate folder labeled "Site 8." Inside was a single map showing an eighth contamination area—not in

Maplewood Bay, but in the watershed that supplied the town's drinking water.

"He never documented this in his official report," Eliza said, showing Eleanor the map. "This is what Nathan meant about an eighth site."

Eleanor studied the map, her expression grim. "Because this wasn't part of the original experiment. This was added later—after Thomas began raising concerns. Look at the date."

The map was dated two weeks before Thomas Morgan's death.

"They expanded the contamination as retaliation? To ensure the experiment couldn't be shut down?"

"Or to ensure Thomas couldn't expose it without implicating himself further." Eleanor pointed to a notation in the corner. "This is Thomas's handwriting. He discovered Site 8 just before he died."

Eliza continued examining the documents, finding a personal letter from her father, sealed in a separate envelope addressed to "Eliza—When You're Ready."

With slightly trembling hands, she opened it.

My dearest Eliza,

If you're reading this, I am gone, and you have discovered the truth about Project Maplewood. I can only imagine your disappointment and anger. You have every right to both.

I made choices I deeply regret. When Northstar approached me about environmental monitoring for a classified project, I convinced myself it was for the greater good. Controlled exposure, minimal risk, valuable data for national security. The perfect justification for the morally indefensible.

When I realized the true scope of the health impacts, I tried to modify the project from within. Another mistake. By the time I understood that Northstar and their government partners had no intention of stopping—that the data was more valuable to them than the lives affected—I was already complicit.

Your diagnosis was the wake-up call I needed. The project I had helped design had harmed my own child. There could be no more self-deception after that.

I've compiled everything here—all the evidence needed to expose Project Maplewood and hold those responsible accountable. I've made copies and secured them in multiple locations. If something happens to me, others will ensure this information reaches the proper authorities.

I don't ask for forgiveness, only understanding. The man who taught you about justice and integrity—that was the real me, Eliza. The me who finally found the courage to stand against what I had helped create.

I love you more than anything in this world. Whatever you decide to do with this information, know that I believe in you completely.

Dad

Eliza folded the letter carefully, her vision blurring slightly. The complexity of her father—his flaws, his courage, his love—crystallized in those words. He had been part of something terrible, had tried to stop it too late, and had died for that choice.

And now, thirty years later, she held the evidence that could finally expose the truth.

"We need to secure these documents," she said to Eleanor. "Make copies, get them to state authorities and the EPA."

"And the USB drive?"

Eliza examined it—a modern device, not something from thirty years ago. "This must be what Nathan has been adding to the box. His insurance policy."

"Or additional evidence he's collected over the years."

Either way, it would need to be examined carefully, in a secure environment. Eliza placed everything back in the box except for a few key documents she photographed with her phone—insurance against any attempt to intercept them before they reached authorities.

As they prepared to leave, Eleanor placed a hand on Eliza's arm. "Your father made terrible mistakes, but he tried to make them right in the end. That counts for something."

"I know." Eliza managed a small smile. "He taught me that justice isn't about perfection—it's about accountability. About facing the consequences of your actions."

"And now?"

"Now we make sure everyone involved in Project Maplewood finally faces theirs."

The black sedan was waiting outside the bank, parked across the street with its engine running. As Eliza and Eleanor emerged with the safe deposit box contents secured in Eliza's messenger bag, the vehicle's door opened.

A man stepped out—tall, military bearing, nondescript dark clothing. The same figure who had delivered the photograph to Eliza's apartment. He made no move toward them, simply stood watching, his presence a clear message: We know what you have.

Eliza guided Eleanor toward her car, maintaining situational awareness. "Don't react, but we're being watched. Black sedan across the street."

"I see it," Eleanor replied calmly. "Federal agent, if I had to guess. DoD or intelligence community."

"Friend or foe?"

"With this level of classification? Neither. Just someone protecting government interests."

They reached Eliza's car without incident. As they drove away, the black sedan pulled into traffic several cars behind them—following but not pursuing.

"We're being tailed," Eliza noted, checking the rearview mirror.

"Expected. The question is, what do they want? To recover the documents, or to ensure they reach the right authorities?"

"Only one way to find out." Eliza made a series of turns, confirming the sedan stayed with them at a consistent distance. Not aggressive, but persistent. "They're not trying to stop us. Just monitoring."

"Which suggests they might prefer official channels handle this. Less messy than direct intervention."

Eliza considered their options. The documents needed to be secured and copied before being submitted to authorities. But with unknown parties watching, any stop they made could be compromised.

"We need a secure location," she said. "Somewhere to review everything properly before deciding next steps."

"My hotel room is out. Too easily accessed."

"And my apartment's been compromised." Eliza thought for a moment. "But I know somewhere they wouldn't expect."

She took a circuitous route through town, using traffic patterns disrupted by storm cleanup to her advantage. Eventually, she pulled into the parking lot of Maplewood Bay Memorial Hospital.

"James's room," Eleanor realized. "Smart. Public building with security, multiple exits, and they won't expect us to bring classified documents to a hospital."

"Exactly. And James has a secure laptop we can use to check the USB drive."

They entered through the main entrance, taking the elevator to the fourth floor. The black sedan remained in the parking lot, its occupant apparently content to wait.

James was sitting up in bed when they arrived, his laptop open on the adjustable table. He raised an eyebrow at Eleanor's presence but made no comment.

"We got the documents," Eliza said without preamble. "Everything my father compiled about Project Maplewood, plus whatever Nathan's been adding to the box."

"And we're being watched," Eleanor added, closing the door behind them. "Black sedan, federal type."

"I saw it pull in after you," James confirmed. "Been monitoring the hospital security feed." He gestured to his laptop, which showed various camera views of the building entrances. "Our friend is still in the car, making calls."

Eliza spread the key documents on James's bed, giving him a quick summary of what they'd found. His expression darkened as he absorbed the implications.

"This goes beyond Maplewood Bay," he said, examining the authorization forms. "DoD, intelligence agencies, pharmaceutical companies developing chemical weapons under the guise of 'non-lethal deterrents.' Using an entire town as a test site."

"And local officials who allowed it," Eleanor added. "For money, power, whatever they were offered."

"The question is, what do we do with it?" Eliza gestured to the documents. "Official channels could bury this again. These signatures include people who are now in very high positions."

"But going outside channels makes us targets," James countered. "More so than we already are."

Eleanor, who had been examining the USB drive, spoke up. "Before we decide, we should see what's on this. It might change our calculus."

James connected the drive to his laptop, running a security scan before opening it. The drive contained hundreds of files, meticulously organized by date and subject.

"Nathan's insurance policy," he confirmed, scrolling through the contents. "Recordings, photographs, internal memos—he's been documenting everything for decades. Including conversations with his co-conspirators."

He played a sample recording—Nathan and Wallace discussing the "containment" of Sarah Lindstrom, the fifth victim. Their casual planning of her disappearance was chilling in its detachment.

"This is enough to convict them both of murder," Eliza said. "But why would Nathan keep evidence that incriminates himself?"

"Leverage," Eleanor suggested. "Insurance against his partners deciding he was expendable."

"And now he's using it as leverage with us," James added. "Offering a full accounting in exchange for... what? Leniency? Witness protection?"

"Whatever he wants, these documents and recordings need to reach authorities who can't be influenced by the people named in them." Eliza began sorting the physical documents, separating them by type and significance. "State Attorney General, FBI, EPA, and media outlets simultaneously. Too many targets to suppress them all."

"I have contacts at the Boston Globe," Eleanor offered. "People who can't be easily intimidated."

"And I know an FBI agent in the public corruption unit," James added. "Someone I trust."

As they formulated a plan for distributing the evidence, Eliza's phone rang—an unknown number. She answered cautiously.

"Detective Morgan." The voice was male, professional, unfamiliar. "I believe you have materials of interest to national security."

"Who is this?"

"Someone who shares your interest in justice for the victims of Project Maplewood. My colleagues and I have been monitoring the situation for some time."

"The black sedan."

"A necessary precaution. We needed to confirm you had accessed the documents before making contact."

"And now?"

"Now we would like to offer assistance in ensuring those documents reach the appropriate authorities without interference."

Eliza put the call on speaker, exchanging glances with James and Eleanor. "Why would you help expose a government-sanctioned project?"

"Because Project Maplewood was never fully sanctioned. It exceeded its authorized parameters, violated multiple laws and ethical guidelines. The individuals responsible have used government connections to shield themselves from accountability for decades."

"And you represent...?"

"A task force established to investigate historical abuses of classified programs. We've been building a case against Project Maplewood's architects for years, but lacked the specific evidence your father compiled."

"Convenient timing," James commented skeptically.

"Not convenience. Opportunity. Nathan Wells's arrest created an opening we've been waiting for. His decision to direct you to the safe deposit box was unexpected but fortuitous."

Eliza considered the offer. It could be legitimate—a faction within the government seeking to clean house. Or it could be an elaborate trap to recover and suppress the evidence.

"If you're serious about justice," she said, "then you won't object to us making our own copies and distributions of these documents before sharing them with you."

A pause. "That would be acceptable, with the understanding that certain technical details of the chemical compounds should be redacted for public safety."

"We'll need verification of your identity and authority."

"Of course. My credentials can be verified through official channels. I suggest the State Attorney General's office as a neutral intermediary."

The conversation continued, establishing parameters for a meeting later that day with representatives from multiple agencies. Eliza insisted on conditions that would ensure their safety and the security of the evidence—public location, multiple witnesses, simultaneous distribution to media outlets.

After ending the call, she turned to James and Eleanor. "Thoughts?"

"Cautious optimism," James replied. "They could have simply tried to take the documents by force. The fact that they're negotiating suggests legitimacy."

"Or a more sophisticated trap," Eleanor countered. "But I agree it's worth pursuing, with appropriate safeguards."

Eliza nodded, her decision made. "We proceed as planned. Make copies, arrange for simultaneous distribution to multiple authorities and media outlets. If this task force is legitimate, they'll work within those parameters."

As they prepared the documents for copying and distribution, Eliza found herself returning to her father's letter. The man who had helped create Project Maplewood and the man who had tried to expose it—both versions were true. Both were part of his legacy.

And now, completing what he had started thirty years ago would be part of hers.

The truth about Maplewood Bay—about the experiment that had poisoned its residents, about the conspiracy that had silenced whistleblowers, about her father's role in both—would finally be revealed.

Whatever came next, there would be no more silence. Only echoes of a truth too long buried.

Chapter 9: The Reckoning

The State Attorney General's office occupied the top three floors of a modern glass building in downtown Portland, Maine. Eliza Morgan, James Harlow, and Eleanor Chen arrived precisely at the agreed time, escorted by state troopers who had met them at a public location and verified their identities.

The conference room where the meeting would take place had been swept for surveillance devices and secured. Representatives from multiple agencies were already present: the State Attorney General herself, two FBI agents from the public corruption unit, an EPA investigator, and the man from the black sedan—who introduced himself as Special Agent Daniel Reeves, Department of Justice, Special Investigations Division.

"Thank you for coming," the Attorney General began, her expression grave. "I understand you have evidence regarding a classified project conducted in Maplewood Bay over the past thirty years."

"Evidence of illegal human experimentation, environmental crimes, and multiple murders to cover it up," Eliza confirmed, placing her messenger bag on the table. "Before we proceed, I want confirmation that copies of these documents have been received by the media outlets we specified."

Agent Reeves nodded to an assistant, who displayed confirmation receipts on a screen. "The Boston Globe, Washington Post, and ProPublica have all received and acknowledged receipt of the encrypted files. They will unlock them with the key you provided if they don't receive a safety confirmation from you within two hours."

It was a necessary precaution—insurance against any attempt to suppress the evidence once it was in government hands. Eliza had insisted on it, and to her surprise, Agent Reeves had readily agreed.

"Now," the Attorney General said, "please walk us through what you've discovered."

For the next hour, Eliza, James, and Eleanor methodically presented the evidence from Thomas Morgan's safe deposit box and Nathan Wells's USB drive. They explained the origins of Project Maplewood, its expansion beyond authorized parameters, the deliberate contamination of seven sites around town, and the conspiracy to silence anyone who threatened to expose it.

The officials listened intently, occasionally asking clarifying questions but mostly allowing the presentation to unfold. When they reached the evidence of Nathan's recordings—the casual planning of murders, the manipulation of local authorities, the decades of cover-up—the room grew noticeably tenser.

"This goes beyond what we suspected," Agent Reeves admitted. "We've been investigating allegations of unauthorized human testing from several classified Cold War-era programs, but the scope and duration of Project Maplewood exceeds anything we've documented."

"And the local officials involved?" the Attorney General asked.

"Chief Wallace and Mayor Whitaker were active participants," James explained. "Wallace was originally Northstar's head of security before joining the police force. Whitaker received financial compensation for facilitating zoning approvals that allowed the project to operate undetected."

"What about current federal officials?" one of the FBI agents asked. "These authorization forms include signatures from individuals who now hold significant positions."

"That's why we insisted on media distribution," Eleanor said firmly. "To ensure accountability regardless of political connections."

The discussion continued, focusing on immediate next steps: securing arrest warrants for Wallace and Whitaker, coordinating with EPA for emergency assessment of the contamination sites, establishing a health monitoring program for affected residents, and preparing for the inevitable public disclosure once the media published their stories.

Throughout the meeting, Eliza found herself watching Agent Reeves. His willingness to expose a government-sanctioned project seemed at odds with his position. When there was a brief break in the proceedings, she approached him directly.

"Why are you helping with this?" she asked quietly. "Most people in your position would be focused on damage control, not accountability."

Reeves considered her for a moment. "My father grew up in Maplewood Bay. Moved away in the seventies, before the project started. But his brother—my uncle—stayed. Died of a rare neurological condition in 1992. One that's statistically overrepresented in Maplewood Bay residents."

"I'm sorry."

"Don't be. It's what led me to this work. To finding others like me within the system who believe that national security can't be used to justify crimes against our own citizens." He glanced toward the documents spread across the table. "Your father made a mistake getting involved with Project Maplewood. But he tried to make it right. That counts for something."

The same words Eleanor had used. Perhaps there was truth in them.

As the meeting reconvened, the Attorney General outlined the immediate actions her office would take. "We'll coordinate with federal authorities on arrests and evidence collection. Agent Reeves's task force will handle the classified aspects and liaison with defense and intelligence agencies. The EPA will begin emergency assessment of the contamination sites tonight."

"And Nathan Wells?" Eliza asked.

"His cooperation will be taken into consideration," one of the FBI agents replied. "But given his direct involvement in multiple homicides, any deal will be limited. He's looking at significant prison time regardless."

It was a start. Not perfect justice—nothing could truly compensate for thirty years of poisoned lives and silenced voices—but accountability at last.

As the meeting concluded, Eliza felt a weight lifting. The truth about Maplewood Bay would finally be known. Her father's last act would be completed. The victims would have recognition, if not restoration.

But as they prepared to leave, her phone rang—James Harlow's partner at the Maplewood Bay Police Department.

"Detective Morgan," the officer said, his voice urgent. "There's been a development. Chief Wallace is gone. Left the station about an hour ago after receiving a call. And Mayor Whitaker's security detail reports he's also missing."

Eliza exchanged glances with James. "They know."

"There's more," the officer continued. "Nathan Wells escaped custody during transport to the county facility. The transport vehicle was found abandoned, both deputies unconscious but alive."

The weight that had lifted settled back, heavier than before. The three principal conspirators were loose—and almost certainly aware that their decades of secrets were about to be exposed.

"We need to move now," Eliza told the assembled officials. "Wallace and Whitaker will be desperate. They might try to destroy evidence, silence remaining witnesses—"

"Or flee the country," Agent Reeves finished. "We'll coordinate with border patrol, airport security, and coast guard. If they're trying to run, we'll intercept them."

"And if they're not running?" James asked. "If they're planning something else?"

No one had an immediate answer. But Eliza felt a cold certainty forming. "The documents," she said. "My father's report identified seven contamination sites. Nathan claimed there was an eighth that my father never documented—the town's water supply."

"Which we've confirmed from the safe deposit box materials," the EPA investigator noted.

"But what if there's a ninth?" Eliza continued, the pieces connecting in her mind. "A failsafe. Insurance against exposure."

"What kind of failsafe?" the Attorney General asked.

"I don't know exactly. But Nathan's recordings include conversations about 'Protocol Omega'—a contingency plan if Project Maplewood was ever exposed. Something that would make public disclosure impossible or irrelevant."

Agent Reeves was already on his phone, issuing orders. "We need to locate Wells, Wallace, and Whitaker immediately. Full surveillance activation, all available personnel."

"I'm going back to Maplewood Bay," Eliza decided. "Whatever they're planning, it will center there."

"I'm coming with you," James said, rising despite his injured leg.

"As am I," Eleanor added. "I know the original chemical compounds better than anyone here. If they're planning to use them somehow, you'll need my expertise."

The Attorney General nodded. "Go. We'll coordinate from here, provide whatever support you need. But Detective Morgan—" she fixed Eliza with a serious look, "—this is now an official multi-agency operation. Follow protocols. No lone-wolf actions."

Eliza nodded, though they both knew it was a promise that circumstances might force her to break.

The drive back to Maplewood Bay was tense, the three of them mostly silent as they processed the implications of the escaped conspirators. Agent Reeves maintained regular contact, updating them on the search efforts, but so far there was no sign of Wells, Wallace, or Whitaker.

"They'll be together," James said as they approached the town limits. "They need each other now. Wallace has the tactical knowledge, Whitaker the political connections, and Nathan the scientific expertise."

"But what are they planning?" Eleanor wondered. "Even if they eliminate us, the evidence is already distributed. The media will publish within hours."

"Unless they create a bigger story," Eliza said quietly. "Something that overshadows the exposure of a decades-old experiment."

The implication hung in the air, too terrible to voice directly. But they were all thinking it: What if Protocol Omega involved a larger contamination event? A final experiment that would render the town uninhabitable, destroying evidence and creating a disaster that would overwhelm any story about historical wrongdoing?

As they entered Maplewood Bay, the aftermath of the storm was still evident—crews working to clear debris, repair power lines, pump out flooded areas. The town felt vulnerable, its defenses already compromised by nature before this new threat emerged.

Eliza's phone rang—Agent Reeves again.

"We've got something," he said without preamble. "Security camera at the marina captured Wallace's vehicle thirty minutes ago. He appeared to be heading toward the old Northstar research facility."

"The abandoned building on the north shore?" Eliza asked. "I thought that was decommissioned decades ago."

"Officially, yes. But Nathan's files suggest it remained operational in a limited capacity. Some kind of monitoring station for the contamination sites."

"We're heading there now," Eliza decided, already changing direction.

"Backup is en route," Reeves assured her. "State police tactical team, twenty minutes out. Wait for them, Detective."

"We'll assess the situation and proceed accordingly," she replied diplomatically, ending the call before he could press the point.

James gave her a knowing look. "We're not waiting, are we?"

"Twenty minutes could be too long. If they're implementing Protocol Omega, we need to stop them now."

"And if it's a trap?" Eleanor asked.

"Then springing it might be our best chance to capture them."

The old Northstar facility sat on a rocky promontory overlooking the bay, its weathered exterior belying the cutting-edge research once conducted inside. The main gate hung open, the security booth empty. Wallace's police cruiser was parked haphazardly near the entrance, alongside a town government vehicle—Whitaker's—and a nondescript sedan that likely belonged to Nathan.

They parked a discreet distance away and approached on foot, using the overgrown landscaping as cover. The facility appeared deserted at first glance, but a faint light glowed from windows on the ground floor.

"Main entrance is too exposed," James whispered, gesturing to the front doors. "There must be a service entrance."

Eleanor nodded. "East side. I remember from when Thomas brought me here once, years ago."

They circled the building cautiously, finding the service entrance just as Eleanor had indicated. The door was ajar—another sign that their quarry had entered this way and expected no interruption.

Eliza drew her service weapon, James following suit. Eleanor, unarmed, stayed slightly behind them as they entered the building.

The interior was a time capsule—1980s-era research equipment covered in dust sheets, abandoned workstations, faded safety posters on the walls. But unlike truly abandoned buildings, there was an underlying hum of electricity, suggesting some systems remained operational.

They followed a trail of disturbed dust through corridors and laboratories until they reached what appeared to be a central control room. Voices drifted from within—three distinct speakers engaged in urgent conversation.

"The primary system is still functional," Nathan's voice, clinical and detached. "But the secondary triggers will need manual activation."

"How long?" Wallace, impatient.

"Thirty minutes to bring everything online. Another ten to synchronize the release mechanisms."

"And the coverage area?" Whitaker, his politician's voice strained with stress.

"As discussed. The entire town and surrounding watershed. Enough contamination to render the area uninhabitable for decades. By the time anyone can safely investigate, all evidence of Project Maplewood will be chemically degraded beyond recognition."

Eliza exchanged horrified glances with James and Eleanor. Their worst fears confirmed— Protocol Omega was indeed a scorched-earth contingency, designed to eliminate both evidence and witnesses through catastrophic contamination.

She gestured for them to hold position, then used her phone to silently message Agent Reeves: Confirmed. Protocol Omega is mass contamination event. Facility operational. Need immediate evacuation order for town.

His reply came seconds later: Understood. Evacuation protocols initiating. Tactical team 15 minutes out. DO NOT ENGAGE.

But the conversation from the control room made it clear they didn't have 15 minutes.

"Systems coming online," Nathan announced. "Containment vessels pressurizing."

"What about the evacuation order?" Whitaker asked. "If we're going to maintain the industrial accident cover story, we need to at least appear to warn people."

"Timing is critical," Wallace replied. "Order goes out ten minutes before release—enough to create panic and confusion, not enough for effective evacuation. The chaos will only help sell the accident narrative."

"And our extraction?" Whitaker again, clearly concerned about his own survival.

"Helicopter landing in twenty minutes on the roof," Wallace assured him. "We'll be well clear before the primary release."

Twenty minutes. The tactical team wouldn't arrive in time. The conspirators would escape, and Maplewood Bay would become a toxic wasteland—all to protect the secrets of three men who had already caused incalculable harm.

Eliza made her decision. She signaled to James, indicating they would enter from opposite sides of the doorway. Eleanor would stay back, protected but ready to provide technical expertise if needed.

On a silent three-count, they moved.

"Police! Freeze!" Eliza shouted, entering the control room with her weapon trained on the three men.

The room was larger than expected, filled with monitoring equipment, chemical storage units, and a central control console where Nathan stood. Wallace and Whitaker flanked him, both turning in surprise at the intrusion.

Wallace recovered first, his hand moving toward his sidearm.

"Don't," James warned from the opposite doorway, his weapon steady despite his injured leg. "Hands where we can see them. All of you."

For a tense moment, it seemed Wallace might risk it. But Whitaker raised his hands immediately, his political instincts for self-preservation overriding any loyalty to his co-conspirators. Nathan remained focused on the console, his hands still on the controls.

"Step away from the console, Dr. Wells," Eliza ordered.

"You don't understand what you're interrupting," Nathan replied, not looking up. "The system is already initializing. The chemical synthesis has begun."

"Then shut it down."

"It's not that simple." Now he did look up, his expression oddly calm. "Protocol Omega was designed to be irreversible once initiated. A dead man's switch, if you will."

"He's lying," Eleanor said, entering the room despite the danger. "Every chemical process has abort parameters. Thomas would have insisted on it."

Nathan's eyes widened slightly at Eleanor's appearance. "Dr. Chen. I didn't expect to see you again after all these years."

"Evidently not. Now tell us how to shut down the protocol."

While they spoke, Wallace was subtly shifting position, moving away from the console toward a side door. James tracked him with his weapon, but his attention was divided between Wallace and the ongoing confrontation.

"The abort sequence requires biometric confirmation from two primary researchers," Nathan explained. "Thomas Morgan was one. I'm the other. Without Thomas, the system cannot be aborted."

"You're still lying," Eleanor challenged. "Thomas would never design a system that couldn't be overridden in an emergency. He was methodical about failsafes."

A flicker of something—respect, perhaps—crossed Nathan's face. "You knew him well. You're right, of course. There is an emergency override. But it requires direct access to the primary containment vessels and manual venting of the precursor chemicals. Dangerous work, potentially fatal exposure."

"Where are the containment vessels?" Eliza demanded.

Nathan hesitated, then nodded toward a heavy door at the rear of the control room. "Sublevel two. But I strongly advise against—"

The rest of his sentence was cut off by sudden movement. Wallace, seeing an opportunity in the distraction, lunged for the side door. James fired a warning shot, the bullet embedding in the wall inches from Wallace's head.

"Next one won't miss," James promised.

But the warning shot created the chaos Wallace had hoped for. Whitaker dropped to the floor in panic, and Nathan used the distraction to activate something on the console—a secondary control sequence that caused red warning lights to flash throughout the facility.

"What did you do?" Eliza demanded, keeping her weapon trained on him.

"Accelerated the timeline," Nathan replied calmly. "The primary release will now occur in ten minutes, not forty. Enough time for us to reach the helicopter, not enough for you to stop the process."

"You'll kill everyone in town," Eleanor said, horrified. "Including yourself if you don't reach that helicopter in time."

"A calculated risk. But necessary to protect the greater good."

"What greater good?" Eliza challenged. "Protecting yourselves from accountability?"

"Protecting national security," Wallace interjected. "The technologies developed through Project Maplewood have applications far beyond what you can imagine. Military, intelligence—capabilities that give our country critical advantages."

"At the cost of poisoning your own community for thirty years," James countered. "Killing anyone who threatened to expose you."

"Acceptable losses for national security," Wallace insisted, his true priorities finally revealed.

Eliza made a swift decision. "James, keep them covered. Eleanor, come with me. We're going to manually abort the release."

"You can't!" Nathan protested. "The exposure will kill you!"

"Then give us the protection protocols," Eleanor demanded. "The facility must have emergency equipment for chemical containment."

Nathan hesitated, clearly calculating his options. Finally, he nodded toward a storage locker. "Hazmat suits. Designed for brief exposure to the compounds. They won't provide complete protection, but they might buy you enough time."

"Eliza, this is insane," James objected. "Wait for the tactical team."

"They won't arrive in time. And I'm not letting these three sacrifice an entire town to save themselves." She turned to Eleanor. "You don't have to come. This isn't your fight."

"It became my fight thirty years ago when they killed Thomas," Eleanor replied firmly. "I'm coming."

They retrieved the hazmat suits from the locker—full-body protection with integrated breathing apparatus. As they donned the equipment, Eliza kept one eye on the three conspirators, still held at gunpoint by James.

"The manual override requires simultaneous venting of all seven primary containment vessels," Nathan explained, his tone suggesting he still believed the attempt would fail. "The venting controls are color-coded. You must release them in sequence—blue, green, yellow, red, purple, orange, black. Any deviation will trigger immediate release."

"And we trust this information why?" James asked skeptically.

"Because despite everything, I don't actually want to die today," Nathan replied. "If they succeed, we all survive to face whatever justice awaits us. If they fail, none of us leaves this facility alive."

It wasn't exactly reassuring, but it had the ring of truth. Self-preservation had always been Nathan's primary motivation.

With the hazmat suits secured, Eliza and Eleanor prepared to enter the sublevel. The facility's warning system continued to flash red, a digital countdown on the main console showing just under nine minutes remaining.

"If we're not back in eight minutes, get out," Eliza told James. "Get clear of the facility and make sure the evacuation is proceeding."

"I'm not leaving without you," he insisted.

"That's an order, Detective Harlow."

Their eyes met through the clear visors of their hazmat suits, a world of unspoken feelings passing between them. Finally, James nodded. "Eight minutes. Not a second longer."

Eliza turned to the three conspirators. "When this is over, you're facing charges for every life you've destroyed over thirty years. There won't be any helicopters, any escapes. Just accountability."

"We'll see," Wallace replied, his expression suggesting he hadn't given up on finding a way out.

With that final exchange, Eliza and Eleanor entered the heavy door leading to the sublevels, descending into the heart of Project Maplewood's darkest secret.

Sublevel two was a stark contrast to the abandoned appearance of the upper facility. Here, equipment hummed with active power, monitoring systems displayed current data, and the seven primary containment vessels stood in a circular arrangement around a central control station.

Each vessel was the size of a small car, constructed of reinforced steel with multiple failsafe systems visible on their exteriors. Digital displays showed increasing pressure levels as the chemical synthesis proceeded inside.

"The venting controls," Eleanor said, pointing to a panel on each vessel. Color-coded handles were prominently marked, designed for emergency manual operation.

"Blue first," Eliza confirmed, moving to the appropriate vessel. "Then green, yellow, red, purple, orange, black."

"Exactly in that sequence," Eleanor emphasized. "I'll take the first three, you take the last four. We'll need to coordinate precisely."

They positioned themselves at their assigned vessels, the countdown on a wall-mounted display showing seven minutes remaining. The pressure readings continued to climb, the containment vessels emitting ominous creaking sounds as the chemicals inside reacted.

"On my mark," Eleanor said, gripping the blue handle. "Three, two, one, mark!"

She pulled the blue handle down firmly. A hissing sound emanated from the vessel as pressure began venting through a secured system. Immediately, she moved to the green-handled vessel.

"Green on my mark. Three, two, one, mark!"

The process continued, each vessel venting in sequence. As Eleanor completed the yellow vent,

Eliza took over with the red. The air in the sublevel was becoming visibly hazy despite their sealed suits, suggesting some leakage from the venting systems.

"Red complete," Eliza announced, moving quickly to the purple-handled vessel. "Purple on my mark. Three, two, one, mark!"

As she pulled the handle, an alarm different from the facility warning began to sound. The digital display flashed a new message: CONTAINMENT BREACH DETECTED.

"The suits aren't fully protecting us," Eleanor realized, checking her own suit's integrity monitor. "We're getting exposure."

"Keep going," Eliza insisted, already moving to the orange-handled vessel. "Orange on my mark. Three, two, one, mark!"

This vent produced a more violent reaction, the vessel shuddering as pressure released. The haze in the room was thickening, creating a visible fog that made it difficult to see the final vessel.

"Last one," Eliza said, locating the black-handled vessel through the chemical fog. "Black on my mark. Three, two, one, mark!"

As she pulled the final handle, the entire system emitted a series of loud hisses and mechanical clicks. The wall display changed from countdown to a new message: EMERGENCY ABORT SEQUENCE INITIATED. CONTAINMENT NEUTRALIZATION IN PROGRESS.

"We did it," Eleanor said, her voice weak even through the communication system in their suits. "The chemicals are being neutralized."

But their success came with a cost. Both of their suit integrity monitors were now flashing red warnings. The exposure levels were climbing despite the protection, the specialized compounds designed by Project Maplewood penetrating even the hazmat materials.

"We need to get out," Eliza urged, taking Eleanor's arm to guide her through the thickening chemical fog. "Back to the control room."

They staggered toward the exit, their movements becoming increasingly uncoordinated as the chemical exposure affected their nervous systems. The door to the stairwell seemed impossibly far away, the distance stretching with each labored step.

"Thomas would be proud," Eleanor managed, her breathing audibly strained. "You finished what he started."

"We both did," Eliza replied, fighting to keep them moving forward. "Stay with me, Eleanor. We're almost there."

They reached the stairwell just as Eliza's vision began to blur around the edges. The climb back to the control level was excruciating, each step requiring conscious effort as their bodies fought the chemical effects.

When they finally pushed through the door into the control room, they found a changed situation. The tactical team had arrived, its members securing Wallace and Whitaker in handcuffs. Nathan was still by the console, now under the direct supervision of Agent Reeves.

James rushed to them as they stumbled into the room, helping to remove their contaminated hazmat suits with the assistance of tactical team members in their own protective gear.

"Decontamination protocols now!" he shouted. "They've been exposed!"

What followed was a blur for Eliza—emergency medical personnel, decontamination procedures, oxygen masks, and urgent conversations about antidotes and treatment protocols. Through it all, she was aware of Eleanor beside her, receiving the same urgent care, and of

James refusing to leave her side despite orders to clear the area.

As the immediate crisis response stabilized, Agent Reeves approached their treatment area. "The abort sequence worked," he confirmed. "The chemicals have been neutralized. No release occurred."

"The town?" Eliza asked through her oxygen mask.

"Evacuation proceeding as a precaution, but no contamination detected beyond this facility. You stopped it in time."

Relief washed through her, temporarily overwhelming even the effects of the chemical exposure. They had prevented Protocol Omega. Maplewood Bay was safe.

"And them?" She nodded toward where Wallace, Whitaker, and Nathan were being processed by federal agents.

"In custody. Facing multiple federal charges—conspiracy, murder, environmental crimes, unauthorized human experimentation. They won't see freedom again."

It was over. Thirty years of secrets, of deaths disguised as accidents, of an entire town unknowingly part of an illegal experiment—all exposed at last. Justice for Sarah Lindstrom and the other victims. Justice for her father.

As medical personnel prepared to transport them to a specialized treatment facility, Eliza reached for James's hand. "The documents," she said. "Make sure they're secured. All of it needs to be public."

"Already happening," he assured her. "The media received the decryption keys when we didn't check in. By tomorrow, everyone will know the truth about Project Maplewood."

"And the town? The people who've been exposed for years?"

"The Attorney General is establishing a victim compensation fund. Health monitoring, treatment programs, financial support. It won't fix everything, but it's a start."

Eliza nodded, too exhausted to speak further. As they were loaded into ambulances, she caught a final glimpse of Nathan Wells being led away by federal agents. Their eyes met briefly across the room—the man who had been part of her father's death, who had continued the experiment for decades afterward, who had been willing to sacrifice an entire town to avoid accountability.

In that moment, she saw something unexpected in his expression. Not defiance or calculation, but a weary acceptance. Perhaps even a flicker of relief that it was finally over.

The doors of the ambulance closed, and Eliza surrendered to the exhaustion and chemical effects, knowing that when she woke, the world would be different. The truth about Maplewood Bay would no longer be silenced.

The echo of that silence had finally been broken.

Chapter 10: The Aftermath

Three months after the exposure of Project Maplewood, Eliza Morgan stood at the edge of Maplewood Bay, watching the sunset paint the water in shades of gold and crimson. The marina had been transformed—not just by repairs following the storm, but by the extensive decontamination efforts that had followed the revelations about the thirty-year experiment.

EPA teams in hazmat suits had become a common sight around town, methodically testing and treating each of the seven contamination sites identified in Thomas Morgan's original report. The eighth site—the water supply—had required the most extensive intervention, with temporary water systems established while the permanent infrastructure underwent decontamination.

The physical recovery of Maplewood Bay was well underway. The emotional recovery would take much longer.

Eliza's own recovery had been challenging. The chemical exposure during the abort sequence at the Northstar facility had left both her and Eleanor with lingering health effects—periodic neurological symptoms, respiratory issues, heightened sensitivity to certain environmental triggers. The specialized medical team overseeing their treatment was cautiously optimistic about eventual improvement, but had been honest about the likelihood of some permanent effects.

A small price to pay for preventing Protocol Omega and saving the town.

She heard footsteps on the newly rebuilt boardwalk behind her and turned to see James Harlow approaching, his limp less pronounced than it had been immediately after his injury. He carried two cups of coffee, offering one to her as he joined her at the railing.

"Thought I might find you here," he said. "Big day tomorrow."

"The first day of the public hearings," Eliza nodded, accepting the coffee. "Hard to believe it's finally happening."

The congressional hearings into Project Maplewood had been scheduled after months of preliminary investigations, evidence gathering, and legal maneuvering. Eliza, James, and Eleanor would all testify, along with dozens of other witnesses—former Northstar employees, government officials involved in the original authorization, medical experts documenting the health impacts, and residents of Maplewood Bay whose lives had been affected by the contamination.

"Nervous?" James asked.

"About testifying? No. About seeing Nathan, Wallace, and Whitaker again? Maybe a little."

The three principal conspirators had been held in federal custody since their arrest, denied bail due to the severity of the charges and the risk of flight. Tomorrow would be the first time Eliza would see them in person since that day at the Northstar facility.

"They can't hurt anyone anymore," James reminded her. "Their power came from secrecy, and that's gone."

It was true. The media coverage following the release of Thomas Morgan's documents and Nathan's recordings had been extensive and unrelenting. Project Maplewood had become a national scandal, prompting investigations into other classified programs, resignations from several high-ranking officials implicated in the cover-up, and a broader conversation about government transparency and accountability.

"I know," Eliza said. "It's not fear, exactly. Just... awareness of unfinished business."

James nodded, understanding without needing further explanation. Despite all that had been revealed, there were still questions without complete answers. The full extent of the government's knowledge and involvement. The total number of victims over thirty years. The long-term health implications for the town's residents.

Some of those questions might be answered during the hearings. Others might never be fully resolved.

"How's your mother doing with all this?" James asked after a comfortable silence.

"Better than I expected. Learning the truth about my father—that he tried to stop the project, that he died trying to expose it—has brought her a kind of peace. She's even talking about writing a memoir about their life together."

"And you? Has it brought you peace?"

Eliza considered the question, watching a fishing boat return to harbor as the light faded. "Not peace, exactly. Understanding, maybe. Acceptance of the complexity. My father made terrible mistakes, but he tried to make them right. That's something I can live with."

James's hand found hers on the railing, a gesture that had become familiar over the past months. Their relationship had evolved gradually as they recovered from their respective injuries and navigated the aftermath of Project Maplewood's exposure. Neither had rushed to define it, content to let it develop naturally amid the chaos of investigations, medical treatments, and media attention.

"Eleanor's flight gets in at nine tomorrow," Eliza said, changing the subject. "She's staying at the Harborview Hotel again."

"I've arranged for a car to pick her up," James replied. "She shouldn't have to deal with transportation after that long flight from Florida."

Eleanor had returned to her retirement home after her medical condition stabilized, but had remained deeply involved in the investigation and preparation for the hearings. Her expertise in both medical examiner procedures and chemical compounds had proven invaluable to the prosecutors building cases against the conspirators.

"She's bringing copies of my father's original research notes," Eliza added. "The ones from before Project Maplewood, when he was still focused on legitimate environmental protection. She thinks they might help establish his true character during the hearings."

"Smart. Humanizing him will be important."

The sun had nearly disappeared below the horizon now, the water darkening to deep indigo. Lights were coming on along the shoreline, including the newly restored lighthouse at the harbor entrance—a symbol of Maplewood Bay's resilience and renewal.

"We should head back," Eliza suggested. "Early start tomorrow."

As they walked along the boardwalk toward town, they passed the memorial that had been erected near the marina entrance—a simple stone marker with the names of all known victims of Project Maplewood. Sarah Lindstrom. Thomas Morgan. Five others whose disappearances had been linked to the conspiracy. And a dedication to "those who suffered in silence, their health and lives compromised by three decades of environmental contamination."

Eliza paused briefly at the memorial, as she often did when passing. A ritual of remembrance and respect. James waited patiently, understanding its importance to her.

They continued into town, where signs of both physical reconstruction and community healing were evident. Businesses reopened after storm damage repairs. New health monitoring centers established to track and treat residents affected by the contamination. Community support groups meeting in the library and church halls.

Maplewood Bay was changing, transforming from a town built on secrets to one committed to truth and accountability. It wouldn't be easy or quick, but it had begun.

The congressional hearing room was packed beyond capacity, with overflow rooms established for additional observers and media. Cameras broadcast the proceedings live to a national audience, the public interest in Project Maplewood undiminished three months after its initial exposure.

Eliza, James, and Eleanor sat together in the witness area, reviewing their prepared statements one final time before being called to testify. Across the room, separated by security personnel, sat Nathan Wells, James Wallace, and Richard Whitaker—each accompanied by defense attorneys, each wearing prison jumpsuits rather than their former professional attire.

The contrast between their current appearance and their former positions of authority was striking. Wallace, once the imposing police chief, seemed diminished without his uniform and badge. Whitaker, the polished politician, appeared haggard and unkempt. Only Nathan maintained something of his former demeanor—observant, analytical, detached.

As Eliza watched them, Nathan's gaze met hers across the room. There was no hostility in his expression, no defiance or pleading. Just a weary acknowledgment of their shared history and the inevitability of this moment.

The hearing began with opening statements from the committee chair and ranking member, followed by testimony from government officials involved in the initial investigation after Project Maplewood's exposure. Agent Reeves provided a comprehensive overview of his task force's findings, including evidence of similar unauthorized experiments in other locations—none as extensive or long-lasting as Maplewood Bay, but concerning nonetheless.

When it was Eliza's turn to testify, she approached the witness table with calm determination. The bright lights and cameras faded from her awareness as she focused on telling the truth—about her investigation, about her father's role, about the conspiracy that had poisoned a town for thirty years.

"Detective Morgan," the committee chair began after she was sworn in, "please describe how you first became aware of potential irregularities related to disappearances in Maplewood Bay."

Eliza recounted the discovery of Sarah Lindstrom's cold case file, the pattern she had identified connecting multiple disappearances over decades, and her gradual uncovering of the environmental contamination that linked them all.

"And your father, Thomas Morgan, was involved in this project?" another committee member asked.

"Yes," Eliza replied, her voice steady. "He was initially recruited by Northstar Industries to monitor the environmental aspects of Project Maplewood. When he discovered the true extent of the health impacts, particularly after my own childhood diagnosis with contamination-related asthma, he compiled evidence and prepared to expose the project. He was killed before he could do so."

"Killed by whom?"

"Based on Nathan Wells's recorded conversations and other evidence, the direct order came from James Wallace, who was then head of security for Northstar before joining the police force. But all three principal conspirators were aware of and complicit in the decision."

The questioning continued for nearly two hours, covering every aspect of her investigation and the events at the Northstar facility. Eliza answered with precision and clarity, neither embellishing nor minimizing the facts. When asked about her own exposure to the chemicals during the abort sequence, she described the ongoing health effects without self-pity or dramatization.

James and Eleanor testified next, each adding their perspectives and expertise to the record. Eleanor's testimony about Thomas Morgan's character and intentions was particularly powerful, providing context that humanized him beyond his mistakes.

Throughout their testimony, Eliza was aware of Nathan, Wallace, and Whitaker watching and listening. Wallace appeared increasingly agitated as the evidence against him mounted. Whitaker seemed to shrink further into himself with each damning revelation. Nathan remained impassive, as if observing an experiment rather than his own downfall.

When the three conspirators were finally called to testify, their approaches diverged dramatically.

Wallace attempted to justify his actions on national security grounds, insisting that Project Maplewood had produced valuable intelligence and military applications that had protected American interests. His testimony grew increasingly defensive under questioning, eventually devolving into accusations against the committee itself.

Whitaker opted for contrition, claiming he had been misled about the true nature of the project and had only learned of the murders after the fact. His performance might have been convincing if not for the recorded conversations that directly contradicted his claims of ignorance.

Nathan, in contrast, was clinically honest. He acknowledged his role in designing the chemical compounds, monitoring their effects, and participating in the conspiracy to silence potential whistleblowers. He neither apologized nor attempted to justify his actions, simply presented them as historical facts.

"Dr. Wells," one committee member asked, clearly disturbed by his detachment, "do you feel any remorse for the harm caused to the people of Maplewood Bay?"

Nathan considered the question with scientific precision. "Remorse implies I would make different choices if given the opportunity again. That would require a different value system than the one that guided my decisions for thirty years. I recognized the ethical compromises involved in Project Maplewood, but prioritized scientific advancement and national security applications over individual welfare. That was wrong by most ethical standards, including those this committee represents."

"That doesn't answer the question," the committee member pressed.

"I regret the suffering caused," Nathan clarified. "I accept responsibility for my role in causing it. Whether that constitutes remorse in the sense you're asking is perhaps a question of semantics rather than substance."

His testimony, while disturbing in its clinical detachment, provided the most comprehensive account of Project Maplewood's operations, decision-making processes, and cover-up mechanisms. It would prove invaluable to prosecutors building criminal cases and to the victims seeking compensation.

As the first day of hearings concluded, Eliza found herself unexpectedly face to face with Nathan as he was being escorted from the room. Security personnel moved to intervene, but Eliza indicated it was acceptable.

"You could have escaped that day," she said quietly. "When Wallace and Whitaker were distracted. You chose to stay and provide the abort sequence information."

Nathan studied her with the same analytical gaze he applied to everything. "The experiment had reached its conclusion. Further data collection would have been redundant."

"Is that how you see it? As just an experiment that ended?"

"No," he admitted after a moment. "That's how I justified it to myself for thirty years. But in that moment, watching you and Dr. Chen risk your lives to stop Protocol Omega... I recognized something I had denied. The human cost was never justifiable, regardless of the scientific value."

It wasn't quite remorse, but it was perhaps as close as Nathan Wells could come to it. A recognition, however late, of the fundamental ethical failure at the heart of Project Maplewood.

"Thomas would have testified like you did today," Nathan added unexpectedly. "Honestly, without self-justification. He understood his responsibility."

Before Eliza could respond, security personnel resumed escorting Nathan away. She watched him go, this complex figure who had been both her father's colleague and his betrayer, who had continued the experiment for decades but had also provided the means to stop its final, catastrophic phase.

James joined her as the room gradually emptied. "You okay?"

"Yes," she said, and meant it. "Just thinking about how many versions of truth exist in a story like this. Nathan's clinical detachment. Wallace's nationalist justifications. Whitaker's self-serving revisionism. My father's complicated legacy."

"And your truth?"

"That justice isn't about perfect narratives or clean resolutions. It's about accountability, about facing consequences, about ensuring the harm stops." She gathered her notes from the witness table. "And sometimes, it's about accepting that the people we love can make terrible mistakes and still be worthy of love."

One year after the exposure of Project Maplewood, Eliza Morgan stood at her father's grave, placing fresh flowers beside the headstone. The cemetery overlooked Maplewood Bay, offering a panoramic view of the town that had been both Thomas Morgan's professional failure and his final attempt at redemption.

Much had changed in that year. The criminal trials of Nathan, Wallace, and Whitaker had concluded with guilty verdicts and substantial sentences. The victim compensation fund had distributed its first payments to affected residents. The EPA had certified five of the seven contamination sites as fully remediated, with work continuing on the remaining two.

Eliza's own life had transformed as well. Her health had stabilized, though some effects of the chemical exposure remained. She had testified at multiple trials and hearings, becoming an unexpected public figure in discussions about government transparency and environmental justice.

And she had made peace with her father's complex legacy—the brilliant scientist who had helped design an unethical experiment, the loving father who had tried to protect his daughter and community when he recognized the harm, the flawed man who had died trying to expose the truth.

"I brought something for you," she said softly to the headstone. From her bag, she removed a small metal bird figurine, similar to those left at the crime scenes but crafted by a local artist as a symbol of remembrance rather than threat. "The memorial at the marina was completed yesterday. Your name is there, along with all the others affected by Project Maplewood. Not just as a victim, but as the person who compiled the evidence that eventually exposed it all."

She placed the bird figurine beside the flowers, its metal surface catching the afternoon sunlight.

"The truth about Maplewood Bay is known now," she continued. "No more secrets, no more silence. Just the long process of healing and rebuilding."

A gentle breeze carried the scent of the bay up to the cemetery—cleaner now than it had been in decades, the water gradually purifying as the contamination was removed. In the harbor below, boats moved in and out, residents continuing their lives with new awareness of what had happened but refusing to be defined solely by it.

Eliza heard footsteps on the cemetery path and turned to see James approaching, respectfully keeping his distance to allow her this private moment. They had moved in together six months ago, their relationship deepening amid the challenges of recovery and testimony. Not despite the difficulties, but partly because of them—the shared experience creating a foundation of understanding and trust.

She gave the headstone a final touch, a gesture of both farewell and connection. "I understand now, Dad. The mistakes, the regrets, the attempt to make things right. All of it. And I forgive you."

As she walked away to join James, Eliza felt a sense of completion that had eluded her since beginning this journey. Not closure—the story of Project Maplewood and its impact on Maplewood Bay would continue for generations. But a recognition that this chapter of her own story had reached its natural conclusion.

The conspiracy of silence had been broken. The truth had been spoken. Justice, imperfect but real, had been achieved.

And in that achievement, both Thomas Morgan's legacy and Eliza's own had been defined—not by the mistakes they had made, but by their unwavering commitment to uncovering truth and protecting the vulnerable, whatever the personal cost.

As they walked together toward the cemetery gates, James took her hand. "Ready?"

Eliza looked back once more at her father's grave, then out to the bay beyond, its waters reflecting the clear blue sky. "Yes," she said. "I'm ready."

Ready to move forward into whatever came next, carrying the lessons of Maplewood Bay but no longer defined by its secrets. Ready to build something new from the foundations of truth that had been so painfully established.

The echo of silence had been replaced by the clear sound of truth—resonating not just through Maplewood Bay, but far beyond, touching lives and institutions that had long operated in shadows similar to those that had concealed Project Maplewood.

It wasn't a perfect ending. But it was a beginning built on truth. And for now, that was enough.

THE END

About the Author

Geoffrey Kneller is an acclaimed author of mystery and thriller novels. His unique blend of psychological suspense and atmospheric storytelling has earned him a dedicated following among readers who appreciate intricate plots and complex characters.

Born and raised in a small coastal town similar to Maplewood Bay, Kneller draws inspiration from the hidden secrets of seemingly idyllic communities. His work often explores themes of justice, memory, and the lasting impact of environmental degradation on small towns.

When not writing, Kneller enjoys hiking along coastal trails, researching historical cold cases, and advocating for environmental conservation. He currently lives in New England with his family.

"The Echo of Silence" is his latest work, combining his passion for environmental themes with his trademark suspenseful storytelling.

Contact: geoffreyknellermystery@gmail.com

Reading Group Guide

1. How does Eliza's photographic memory both help and hinder her investigation? In what ways does perfect recall shape her character?

2. The coastal town of Maplewood Bay serves as more than just a setting in the novel. How does the environment itself become a character in the story?

3. Discuss the symbolism of the bird tokens left at each crime scene. What might they represent beyond being a killer's signature?

4. The novel explores themes of environmental justice and corporate responsibility. How do these themes intersect with the central mystery?

5. How does Eliza's relationship with her mother's fiancé, Nathan, evolve throughout the story? What early clues hint at his true nature?

6. The story takes place during a series of coastal storms. How does the weather mirror the emotional and narrative arcs of the characters?

7. Discuss the significance of Eliza discovering her father's involvement in Project Maplewood. How does this revelation change her understanding of her past?

8. The novel explores how secrets can poison a community over generations. What parallels can you draw to real-world environmental cover-ups?

9. How does Geoffrey Kneller build and maintain suspense throughout the novel? Which techniques were most effective?

10. The ending suggests the possibility of a sequel. What unresolved questions would you like to see addressed in a follow-up novel?

A Note from the Author

Dear Reader,

Thank you for joining Detective Eliza Morgan on her journey through the dark secrets of Maplewood Bay. This story grew from my longstanding interest in the intersection of environmental justice and small-town dynamics. While researching this novel, I spent time in several coastal communities affected by industrial contamination, speaking with residents, environmental activists, and local officials. Their stories of resilience in the face of corporate negligence inspired many elements of this narrative.

The character of Eliza Morgan, with her photographic memory, emerged from my fascination with how we process and store traumatic memories. How might perfect recall be both a gift and a burden? What truths might we prefer to forget? I hope "The Echo of Silence" provides not only an engaging mystery but also prompts reflection on how the choices we make today echo through generations to come.

I'd love to hear your thoughts on the story. You can reach me at geoffreyknellermystery@gmail.com.

Until next time,

Geoffrey Kneller

Printed in Great Britain
by Amazon